MW00464753

23
4

A WOMAN IGNORED

A novel by

T. B. Markinson

Published by T. B. Markinson

Visit T. B. Markinson's official website at tbmarkinson.wordpress.com for the latest news, book details, and other information.

Copyright © T. B. Markinson, 2014

Cover Design by Erin Dameron-Hill / EDHGraphics

Edited by Karin Cox

Proofread by Jeri Walker-Bickett

This book is copyrighted and licensed for your personal enjoyment only. All rights reserved. No part of this publication may be reproduced, stored in a retrieval system, or transmitted in any forms or by any means without the prior permission of the copyright owner. The moral rights of the author have been asserted.

This book is a work of fiction. Names, characters, businesses, places, events, and incidents are the product of the author's imagination or are used fictitiously. Any resemblance to actual persons, living or dead, events, or locales is entirely coincidental.

For Cindy.
Everyone should have a friend like you.

CHAPTER ONE

"Lizzie, I think you should sit down." Sarah, my girlfriend—I mean wife (Why can I never remember that?)—motioned to a chair on the opposite side of the room. I did as she instructed.

Sarah, along with her mom Rose, and Maddie, my brother's former fiancée who had ditched him at the altar, sat across from me, staring at me with blank faces. Too blank. They were really trying not to scare the shit out of me. It wasn't working. I started to squirm in my chair like a child sitting in front of the school principal.

"Um, what's going on?" To say I felt uncomfortable would be an understatement.

"We wanted to have a chat with you," explained Sarah with forced nonchalance.

"A chat—oh ..." I didn't finish my thought. I feared one of them was sick. Rose? Cancer? I flashed a concerned smile at Sarah's mom.

"No, dear. This isn't about me, but thanks for assuming that, since I'm the oldest." Rose's narrowed eyes suggested she was still pissed at me for something I had done a few years back. Even though Sarah had forgiven me, Rose clearly hadn't, and I wasn't sure she ever would, not completely. Sarah, an only child, was Rose's sole purpose in life.

I looked away. "So, what is this, an intervention?"

I thought my behavior had been on the up-and-up lately. That hadn't been the case when Maddie first entered our lives a few years ago. The year of my brother's engagement wasn't a stellar year for me. Sarah called it my lost stage. I didn't know what I wanted, and I made some stupid mistakes, including trying to seduce Maddie. Sarah left me, rightfully so, and I had to pull my shit together—fast.

Until Sarah left me, I didn't realize I was madly in love with her. I knew I loved her, but I couldn't see how much, let alone comprehend what life would be like without her. Since winning her back, not a day went by that I didn't thank my lucky stars.

Her mother, however, still seized every opportunity to remind me how fortunate I was to receive her daughter's forgiveness. I took Rose's abuse. If I were Sarah's mom, I would have wanted to kill me as well.

"I wouldn't say an intervention ..." Sarah turned to Maddie for help.

When I'd hit on Maddie, she put me in my place as soon as I made a pass, slapping me across the face—hard. But I knew that she also felt sorry for me. Maddie knew better than most what it was like growing up in the Petrie family. Eventually, Maddie had helped me realize why I had pushed Sarah away.

Since then, all of us had moved past the unfortunate incident and mended our relationship. Thankfully, Rose never held anything against Maddie; I was the only one she glared at menacingly. Sometimes, when only I could hear her, she imitated a car sound: reminding me of her threat that if I ever hurt her daughter again she would run me over with her Cadillac. She made that threat a few years ago; I believed it then, and I still believed it now. Sarah didn't entirely believe me when I said her mother wanted to mow me down. And sometimes I wasn't sure if I'd actually heard Rose revving a car engine, or whether my guilty conscious caused me to imagine it whenever Rose was around. It was difficult to link

Rose—always dressed immaculately, always so put together—with homicidal tendencies.

"Let's just say it's an informational get-together," suggested Maddie, her storm blue eyes twinkling mischievously.

"Yeah, informational." Sarah didn't sound so sure.

Rose gave me a wink, implying I was in for it now. At least someone was enjoying this.

I felt clammy and wondered if my forehead was breaking out in a sweat. I envisioned sitting in a police station, being interrogated by a team of detectives—a light bulb dangling over my head, swinging precariously for added effect.

"Okay, what kind of information involves the three of you sitting across the room staring at me like I'm in trouble?"

"You aren't in trouble," explained Sarah.

"Not yet, at least," said Maddie with a sardonic smile.

"Will someone just tell me what's going on?" I was close to my breaking point, which was never a good thing. I could be an ass when I felt threatened, and I didn't want to take it to that level.

"Lizzie …" Sarah started, and then faltered.

Maddie gave her an encouraging smile.

"Lizzie, I wanted, with the help of Maddie and my mom, to tell you something. Something that I've been wanting for a while."

Wanted? What did she want? She had already convinced me to marry her two years ago and to buy a house together: the two issues that first sent me into the tailspin I explained earlier.

"I want to have a baby."

The room grew silent—the type of silence that fell when a judge walked into a courtroom to pronounce a death sentence.

I opened my mouth, but I couldn't speak. I was fairly certain I had stopped breathing. There I sat, frozen in confusion, words unable to penetrate my feeble mind.

A baby!

What is a baby? Think, Lizzie! You can figure this out. Think! You know what a baby is. For Christ's sake, you have a PhD, admittedly in history rather than biology, but still! Baby—small, right? Cries a lot? Baby!

"Should we get her some water or something?" asked Maddie, obviously concerned, although she never stopped grinning.

"Is she having a stroke?" pondered Rose. The corners of her mouth quivered oddly, making me wonder if she was trying not to smile.

"Lizzie ... Lizzie ..." Sarah rushed over and kneeled down before me. "Sweetheart, it's okay. Are you okay?" She patted my knee.

"Are you fucking insane!" I sputtered.

"Whew! I thought we'd lost you for a moment," declared Maddie, obviously completely satisfied with my response.

"A baby? What would I do with a baby?" I jumped out of my seat and began to pace. "A baby?"

Sarah laughed and returned to her seat. She crossed her legs. One flip-flop swayed, about to fall from her foot. "Love it, of course."

Oh, of course! Love a baby.

Like it was that easy.

"I know this is a big shock for you. That's why we decided to break the news to you together."

I stopped mid-stride and glared at Sarah. My head spun. I slumped back down in my chair.

"I think this is going pretty well, considering," Maddie told Rose.

Rose nodded. "For Lizzie. She's handling it much better than I thought she would."

"I'm still in the room. I can hear you," I said, snarkily.

All three of them sat there grinning, watching me like I was a three-year-old throwing a tantrum.

Maddie turned to Rose. "Pay up."

"Not yet. This isn't over."

"Mom, what did you bet?" Sarah flashed Rose an accusatory stare and crossed her arms, but I could tell there was no real threat. Sarah enjoyed her mother's feistiness, and why not? She was never the brunt of Rose's spiteful comments or stunts.

"I bet her that Lizzie would faint." Rose, not ruffled at all by her daughter's demeanor, glanced in my direction. "From the looks of her, she still might. She doesn't have any color in her face."

I gritted my teeth and forced an angry puff of air out of my mouth. "And how do you suppose we acquire this baby?" I asked Sarah.

"Acquire? Lizzie, we're talking about a baby—a living thing. You don't acquire one like a sack of potatoes." Sarah laughed nervously.

There was much more to this, and I totally feared what was to come. "Are you suggesting what I *think* you're suggesting?"

"By Jove! I think she's coming around," crowed Maddie.

"For the love of God, Sarah. I'm not getting pregnant."

"You!" Sarah screamed, before breaking into hysterical laughter.

Maddie's jaw hit the floor before she immediately joined in the hilarity. Even Rose cackled some.

"Oh, Lizzie, I do love you. But, you are hopelessly and completely clueless." Sarah wiped away some tears. "I would never ask you to do such a thing."

"So, you want to adopt, then?" I pushed. I might be able to live with that.

"No. You're missing the obvious." Maddie eyeballed me as though her stare might force the right idea directly into my stubborn pea-brain.

"Surrogate?" I whispered, as if it was a dirty word or a despicable concept.

"No, silly." Sarah sashayed over to me and sat on my lap.

"I want to get pregnant."

"Oh." I stared, stone-faced. "How?"

"Really, Lizzie? You can't be this stupid."

"Don't underestimate her," said Rose.

I wanted to tell Rose off, but she was right: I was clueless about Sarah's plan.

"Okay, how can I say this? I want to get pregnant using a sperm donor and one of your eggs."

I stood up abruptly, grabbing Sarah before she toppled off my lap entirely and setting her upright. "*My* egg? You want to suck some of my eggs out of *me*. Why would you want *my* egg?" I paced the room again.

"Because I want to have *your* child." Sarah said that like it was the most natural thing in the world.

"B-but, you said it yourself: I'm an idiot ... completely clueless. Why would you want to perpetuate my genes? You've met my family. Hateful people. Despicable." I stopped pacing and set my legs firmly apart. "No. We can't do this to a baby. No one deserves that. Not even a baby." I started pacing again, afraid that if I stood still they'd corner me.

"Not even a baby! You're funny." Maddie turned to Rose. "Pay up. She's not going to faint now. She's far too worked up."

Rose sighed and reached for her purse where it lay on the coffee table.

Sarah stepped into my path. Both hands on the sides of my face, forcing me to stop and stare into her eyes, she whispered, "I love you. I want to have your baby."

Speechless, I stood there, staring into her shining chocolate eyes.

"This is so exciting!" Maddie clapped. "I'm going to be an aunt." She rushed over and threw her arms around us both.

Rose stayed seated, smiling. "And I'm going to be a grandmother."

Sarah grabbed one of my hands and placed it on her stomach. "Just think, we're going to be parents, Lizzie."

I staggered backward. Before the room went dark, I heard Rose say, "Pay up, Maddie." I wasn't positive, but I thought she followed it up with, "Timber!"

* * *

After I recovered from my humiliating fainting spell, Rose and Maddie left us alone. I lay on the couch while Sarah pampered me, fixing me a cup of tea with extra sugar—even if she had lately forced me to forego sugar altogether—placing a pillow under my head, rubbing my forehead. Maybe I should consider fainting more often.

"Are you feeling better?" she asked.

"Yeah. I feel silly, though." I dipped a shortbread cookie into my tea.

"You went down like a ton of bricks." Sarah stole one of my cookies and plunged it into my cup. "Are you ready for your second shock of the day?"

"Second shock? Are you trying to kill me?" I sipped the tea again, thinking she was joking.

"Not just yet. If I wanted to bump you off, I would amp up your life insurance policy first. Then I'd have to wait a few years, so I wouldn't be a suspect." Her expression was deadly serious.

"Very funny, wise guy. You need to stop watching *Law and Order*," I said, hoping she actually was just joshing.

"We're having dinner with Ethan and Lisa in a couple of hours." She said it casually, as though we had dinner with them all the time; Sarah had only met my best friend, Ethan, for the first time at our wedding. Lisa wasn't able to attend, as their daughter, Casey, had fallen ill. Which meant that I, in fact, had never met Lisa either—and now I was having dinner with her this evening.

"You have been busy, haven't you?" I raised an accusatory eyebrow.

"Why, Lizzie, whatever do you mean?" she feigned ignorance.

"Don't act all innocent. First you set me up today—"

"Set you up!" Sarah cut me off. "You make it sound like I framed you for a crime or something."

"I think having me as a parent is a crime—a crime against humanity." I was only partially kidding.

"Oh, stop it. You'll be a great parent." She tried to placate me with one of her winning smiles.

"Oh, please. How did you get Ethan and Lisa to agree to dinner?"

"I just called him and asked."

"That's it? You didn't have to trick him?"

"Trick him? Why would I have to do that? Have you ever considered that it might be nice to have dinner with your best friend and his wife?" Sarah pinned me with a glare, one eyebrow arched.

Baffled, I replied, "I've never met her."

"You've never met Lisa, not in all these years? How long have you known Ethan?"

"We met in grad school, over eight years ago." People skills weren't my strong suit. In the past, on many occasions, I had been accused of being self-involved.

"You continue to shock the hell out of me."

"You say it like it's a bad thing," I winked. "How long do we have before dinner?"

"Two hours." She peered at me suspiciously, leaning closer. Her ample breasts strained against her tight Broncos T-shirt as she eyeballed me. "Why? Are you going to try to squeeze in a bike ride?" She made no attempt to hide her feelings about that, just sat back away from me, one manicured nail picking at the side seam of her jeans, which were even tighter than her tee.

I was an avid bike rider and generally logged at least twenty miles a day, but bike riding was the last thing on my mind. Sarah looked sexy as hell.

"I hadn't considered it, but now that you suggested it ..."

Sarah pinched my side and growled, "Don't be an ass."

"Don't pinch me." I rubbed my side dramatically, even though she had barely touched me.

"God. You can be such a baby sometimes."

"Baby," I repeated quietly to myself.

I must have sounded scared to death, because Sarah placed a loving hand on my cheek. "Are you okay? I didn't mean to startle you again."

"No, it's fine. I'm—"

"I know. You don't handle change all that well. We'll go slow, Lizzie. I promise. Just not too slow. My clock is ticking."

I stood up and extended my hand. "Care to join me in the bedroom?" I asked with a suggestive wink. I knew I must have looked a fool, compared to her. I was the type who wore sweater vests, and sweater-vest people weren't usually associated with sex appeal or charisma.

"I suppose," she joked. "Only if you feel up to it."

"Hey, if you aren't interested, I can still hop on my bike and take that ride." I playfully tossed her hand away and started to march to the garage.

Sarah grabbed my arm and yanked me around, kissing me to both shut me up and lure me back. I considered it the best way to be told off, and she had perfectly mastered this shushing technique.

"And, since you're so worried about my health, I'll let you do all the work this time." I kissed her again cutting off any protest.

* * *

We sat at a table in a new trendy restaurant in Fort Collins: the kind that served the same food as Applebee's or Chili's but gave each dish a fancier name, a sprig of garnish, and a ten-dollar price increase. Sarah's newest fascination was locating *it* restaurants. Ethan and I usually met at the same coffee shop whenever we got together; however, we hadn't met in ages, not since he and his wife adopted their daughter and Sarah and I got hitched. I had the feeling that this dinner was just one weapon in Sarah's ongoing battle to convince me that having children was grand.

"I still can't believe you haven't met Lisa." Sarah placed a napkin in her lap.

I shrugged while I filled her water glass and mine from the fancy water jug on the table and replaced the glass stopper. The joint had ramped up the hip factor by adding slices of cucumber and weird, unidentifiable green twig things to the water. It didn't look appetizing, but I was thirsty enough to give it a try.

"Never really gave Lisa much thought," I shrugged.

"That's so like you."

"Hey, Ethan didn't meet you until our wedding day, and that's only because he was my best man."

When Sarah and I got engaged, Ethan had joked he should be my best man. You should have seen his face when I asked him for real. I didn't subscribe to the notion that a bride should be confined to a maid of honor. Anything goes at a lesbian wedding. Ethan actually cried during his toast—well, we all did. Of course, I later refused to admit that I had cried, too. To this day, I swear I had something in my eye.

"Do you even know what she looks like?" probed Sarah.

"Now how would I know that, given I've never met her?" I pulled my best "don't be an imbecile" face and took a sip of the water, bracing for something horrible. "Hey, this isn't bad. Refreshing, actually." I pulled the glass away from my mouth to inspect it for weird objects swirling inside like sea monkeys. Not seeing anything unusual, I took another swig, enjoying the flavor.

"You've never seen a picture of her?" Sarah ignored my antics with the water.

I wasn't the type to check out social media to find out what people looked like. "Nope." I rubbed my chin, feeling a hair that needed plucking. I tugged at it. I scratched it unsuccessfully. "Ethan showed me a picture of the kid, but not the wife." I wondered if Ethan had a pair of tweezers with him. I knew for a fact that he carried fingernail clippers. Would that work?

"What's the kid look like?"

I whispered, "She's black." Then flashed my *only joking* smile. Sarah knew their child was black; she also knew I didn't give a hoot about race, color, creed, or any other hoopla.

Sarah laughed. "You're impossible. And completely self-involved."

"Oh no, not that one again." I winked.

"You're in a good mood, considering." She ran a finger up my thigh.

"Considering you nearly killed me today with your announcement."

"Come now, it can't have been that much of a surprise. Do you remember when we purchased the house—the real estate lady and I kept searching for a house with a nursery, and one that was close to a school." Sarah looked smug.

"I thought you meant a nursery for plants, and you teach high school—how was I supposed to put those clues together?" I leaned over and gave her a peck on the cheek.

"Careful, you two, you might scare the homophobes." Ethan's voice was louder than normal, slipping into the Southern accent that he typically tightly controlled. A woman sitting nearby pursed her lips, looking downright insulted that Ethan had classified her as a gay basher.

I stood and gave Ethan one of my best "man hugs." Hugging or touching people, besides Sarah, made me extremely uncomfortable.

Ethan stepped to the side and motioned to his wife.

I had expected Ethan's wife to be frumpy, considering all the conversations he and I had engaged in about him not wanting sex with her. He hated body fluids, which made sex an uncomfortable obligation for him, rather than something he enjoyed. Knowing that, I assumed his wife would be ugly as sin, a woman desperate to have a partner, any partner, in her life. I was wrong.

Dead wrong.

I nodded at the stunning, slender redhead who stood before me. Back in my single days, I would have made a complete fool of myself trying to impress Lisa.

Ethan must have sensed my thoughts, because he flashed me a knowing smile.

Sarah came to my rescue. "It's so lovely to meet you, Lisa."

Sarah, who had no issues with hugging or bodily fluids, threw her arms around Lisa, who was about three inches taller, and gave her a welcoming squeeze. I shifted awkwardly from side to side before putting my hand out for a handshake.

Lisa didn't seem insulted at all; she almost looked as if she expected me to be ill at ease. Ethan had prepared her well, no doubt.

I motioned for the waitress, so we could place our drink orders. Sarah ordered two bottles of wine. "I'll be on the wagon soon, so why not?"

"Did you know that on the wagon comes from the days when they hanged people in England? Prisoners were allowed one last drink on the wagon that transported them to the gallows." I smiled, proud of my ability to share such a fascinating and random historical tidbit.

"I take it you dropped the bomb," said Ethan matter-of-factly.

"What is that supposed to mean?" I directed my question to Sarah.

"Only you would refer to having one last drink before being hung, today of all days." Sarah patted my cheek tenderly. "And to answer your question, Ethan: yes. We told her this afternoon."

I whipped my head around to glare at Ethan. "You knew!"

Ethan was nonplussed by my accusation. Over the years, he'd become quite used to my idiocy.

Sarah shook her head at me before turning to Lisa. "You have the most stunning hair. Oh, how I would love to have hair like yours."

Lisa blushed. "I've always wanted straight hair. We should trade. People don't know how hard curly hair can be."

"It takes her hours to get ready each morning." Ethan tsked, but his eyes beamed as he admired his gorgeous wife.

Again, I wasn't expecting that. He obviously loved her. For years, I'd thought he was a miserable man trapped in a horrible marriage; now I knew it was his aversion to fluids that drove him mad, not his wife. Maybe I had been too self-involved. Maybe I still was? How could I not know this about my best friend?

I picked up my menu, disappointed with the selection. I wanted simple, like bangers and mash from my favorite restaurant in Fort Collins. I was excited to see they offered mac and cheese until I saw it came with lobster. Why would I want lobster with mac and cheese? Could I order the mac and cheese and ask them to hold the lobster? No, Sarah would not appreciate that. I opted for the filet mignon. It sounded fancy but essentially was just a hunk of meat with roasted potatoes on the side.

Sarah actually ordered the mac and cheese with lobster and I was relieved I didn't make an ass out of myself by saying, "Hold the lobster, please" like a child. Ethan followed my lead and had the filet. Lisa ordered short rib tacos.

"Oh, I saw Bobby Flay make red chili short rib tacos just the other day on the Food Network, and they looked divine," said Sarah.

I tried not to roll my eyes when she said divine.

"So how did Lizzie take the news?" Ethan grinned.

I could tell he was bursting at the seams to humiliate me.

"Oh,"—Sarah flashed me a devious smile—"as expected. She fainted."

Lisa looked concerned, but Ethan immediately burst into a gale of laughter. Sarah joined in, encouraging Lisa to finally push her concerns aside and laugh along.

I had never enjoyed being the center of attention, especially when I was the brunt of the joke.

My chair scraped the tiles as I stood, somewhat dramatically. "Ethan, let's go out for a smoke."

"Lizzie! You don't smoke," exclaimed Sarah, who occasionally smoked but quit for good recently—right around the time she cut me off from sugar. Were those clues I missed?

"Didn't you tell me the other day that I should pick up some new hobbies? No time like the present." I stormed off.

Ethan joined me outside after a few moments. I sat on a bench in the middle of Old Town and observed the full moon, which illuminated the dark as if we were in a creepy Hitchcock film. The sky in Fort Collins always seemed endless, because no tall buildings obscured the view. I remembered being in New York City a few years back, feeling trapped by the skyscrapers.

Even though it was a beautiful spring night, the town center was deserted, giving me the heebie-jeebies. On occasions like this, I always wondered if the apocalypse had happened without my knowing.

"So, you're going to be a mommy." Ethan pulled out a cigarette and handed me his pack of Marlboro Lights. I didn't intend on actually smoking ... but on second thought, why not give it a go? Ethan bowed slightly to light my cigarette. Inhaling, I waited for the coughing fit, given that was what happened in the movies. I didn't cough; instead, I whacked my chest as if I had a neurological tic.

Ethan placed one foot on the bench and leaned closer. I stared up into his eyes, inquisitive behind his thick glasses.

"I guess so," I replied.

He sat next to me and slid an arm around my shoulders. "I know you're freaking out, and you're trying hard not to, considering your past with Sarah." Ethan gave me a squeeze. "What you're feeling is normal. Give yourself some time."

"What happens if I don't change? How can I do this to a child?" I sucked on the cigarette and then whacked my chest again.

Ethan chuckled. "I've never seen anyone have that reaction to smoking for the first time before." He blew out a perfect smoke ring. "I know you, Lizzie. You're stubborn, selfish, and annoying."

"Thanks for kicking me while I'm down, buddy."

"I wasn't finished. But, deep down, all of those qualities are for show. You're a loving person and you feel weak when you show your true self. You need to learn that's not a weakness but your greatest strength."

I sat there, speechless. The silence was killing me. "Wow, what's in these cigarettes?" I pointed it at him. "Because that's the biggest crock of shit I've heard in some time." I tried to laugh but couldn't.

Ethan ignored my childish attempt to avoid the heart of the matter.

Both of us sat motionless except for our hands, smoking and admiring the moon.

Finally, Ethan stood. "We'd better go back in. Not sure we should leave our wives alone for too long. Who knows what they're plotting?"

As I walked back in, I saw the worry in Sarah's eyes. Ever since we had got back together, I sensed she was constantly waiting for the other shoe to drop—for the old Lizzie to reappear and take over for good. The look in her eye was like a swift kick to the shin.

Ethan, being the perfect Southern gentleman, pulled out my chair. "Well, now. I think Lizzie is a natural at smoking."

Sarah leaned over and sniffed me. "You *did* have a cigarette!"

"Today marks a new beginning." I raised my wineglass. "To getting pregnant!"

Sarah almost fell out of her seat, but she quickly recovered and grabbed her wineglass, clinking it to mine with

"Cheers."

Ethan gave me an encouraging smile and Lisa looked puzzled. I wondered what Ethan had told her about me.

"So how does this work?" asked Ethan, immediately turning three shades of scarlet. "I mean, whose egg are you using?"

I stopped myself from making a joke about Ethan not knowing the first thing about the birds and the bees, considering his troubles.

"Lizzie's egg, of course." Sarah glowed with happiness.

"I heard getting an egg extraction hurts like hell," Ethan said. "More than actual labor." He winked, but it didn't put me at ease.

"Hey now, don't discourage her, Ethan." Sarah swatted his arm as if they were lifelong friends, even though I could count on one hand how many times they had interacted.

I tugged on my shirt collar, feeling stifled and, to be completely honest, terrified. Lisa noticed. I couldn't discern whether she felt sorry for me or for the child.

My child.

Our child.

Shit.

How did this happen?

Looking at Sarah's face I knew how it happened. I loved her more than I thought possible. And no matter what, I was determined to love our child.

Later that night, Sarah opened a bottle of champagne she had put on ice before we left for dinner. The woman was always prepared, yet it still amazed me. Cold nestled over the city, and I lit the fireplace to combat the nip in the air. We sat on the sofa near the fireplace, with Sarah huddled against my chest, sipping the bubbly.

"Thank you, Lizzie."

"For what? Lighting the fire?" I was enjoying the extra pizzazz that pomegranate seeds added to my drink.

"No. For keeping an open mind. I know I took you by

surprise today."

"I'll say. It's been a while since I fainted." I rested my chin on her soft chestnut hair.

"When was the last time? Yes, when we signed the mortgage papers. Later that night you had the worst panic attack, and then—boom!—out cold on the floor." Sarah chuckled over the memory.

"Hey, you don't have to enjoy the memory that much."

Sarah sat up, gazing into my eyes. "Besides the minor incident today, you've handled it much better than I thought you would. You actually seem open to the idea."

"I'm not sure if I'm there yet."

Sarah pulled away from me.

"Wait, don't do that. Come here." My arm over her shoulder pulled her back. "I love you, and I would do anything for you. But you have to understand: I need time to get used to the idea. I have inner demons to battle, mainly my own crappy childhood. I won't lie. I'm petrified."

"And that's exactly why I think you'd make a great mom. You're scared of letting your child down. Not many people feel that way in the beginning, or ever."

"Well, most people don't have our luxury."

"What do you mean?"

"We get to plan when we want to get pregnant. No oopsies. I imagine most parents are scared for different reasons."

"I had thought of that—getting pregnant and then telling you."

"You wouldn't dare! Would you?" Even to me, my voice didn't sound confident.

"Unfortunately, it'd be hard to get one of your eggs without you noticing." She peppered my neck with soft kisses.

"Are you sure you want my egg? Who knows how my genes will play out?"

"Don't worry. We'll use mine for our second child."

I shot off the couch. "Second child!" My heartbeat

skittered like a trapped animal.

Sarah sat on the couch, a mystifying look on her face; then, the most beautiful smile illuminated her eyes, and all of a sudden I felt calm.

"That's my girl." Sarah drained her champagne. "Now take me to bed. Let's put your nervous energy to better use. Enough baby talk for today."

CHAPTER TWO

Since finishing my PhD a few years ago and being technically unemployed, I had woken up early every day, including Sundays. I wasn't the loafing type, not even after I quit teaching. Once I acquired my doctorate, I concentrated on my true passions: research and writing. I published my first book within the first year of not teaching, and I was working on my second. As much as I had loved teaching, I enjoyed researching and writing more. And my trust fund allowed me to do just that.

By five each morning, I was itching to hop out of bed. That morning, Sarah was dead to the world, as usual. She taught high school English, a frustrating and draining job, so I didn't want to disturb her. I knew how much she loved sleeping in on Sundays.

By the time I got on my bike, the sun was making an appearance. The birds were already announcing the start of a beautiful morning. The chill in the early spring air gave me instant goose bumps. No matter, within ten minutes I'd be warm and riding along Poudre River on my favorite bike trail. Not many people were out, so I felt like I had the river to myself. The water gurgled on my right, and on my left I could see a fox scurrying off to bed. Frost speckled the wild grass, the sun illuminating each strand and making the ice glimmer like gold. Only in nature did I feel this relaxed. Not once had the baby issue popped into my mind. It was as if yesterday hadn't happened. All I felt was tranquil.

I didn't notice much of anything—until I realized I was pedaling past Laporte High School. Glancing at my watch, I saw that it was still early, and I was famished. I decided to head up the road and pop into Frankie's for breakfast. The diner's claim to fame was having the best cinnamon rolls in Colorado, and I agreed wholeheartedly.

After locking my bike outside, I slid into a booth in the back. The waitress was obviously a morning person—or was damn good at pretending she was. Her dishwater brown hair was piled high on top of her head in an old lady bun. Makeup caked the cracks of wrinkles, and her leather skin clocked too many hours in the sun.

"What can I git ya, sugar?" Her raspy, smoker's voice belied the youthful flicker in her eyes.

"Tea and a cinnamon roll, please. Oh, can I also have a big glass of ice water?" I shook my empty water bottle.

"Sure. Looks like you can use it. Are you riding through the canyon after this? Now that the weather is warming up, we've seen loads of bicyclists and motorcycles."

I almost shouted yes, but then thought better. It was tempting. I loved riding in the canyon, but I knew that if I avoided Sarah today, of all days, she'd flip out.

"Nah, I'll head home after this. Too many things to do today," I lied. I had nothing to do. Maybe I'd take Sarah to Denver to catch a foreign flick and then head to Sixteenth Street for dinner. I was still adjusting to not being in school. Sure, researching and writing was demanding, but my schedule was mostly determined by me now, not by professors. I enjoyed the freedom. Occasionally, I was invited to colleges and conferences to speak, which satiated the teaching bug that reared its head from time to time.

The waitress nodded and waddled to the beverage area to prepare my tea and water.

I thought I felt my cell phone vibrate in my pocket. Surely I was imagining it. Who in her right mind would be calling me this early on a Sunday? Just to be safe, I pulled out my phone. Sure enough, I had a text message from Sarah. Odd—usually she called.

"Where are you?"

I texted that I was at Frankie's, having a cup of tea.

"I'll meet you there."

I read the text a couple more times. Why was Sarah up this early on a Sunday? Did she think I was freaking out about yesterday? Actually, I was feeling pretty smug about it. Sure, I had fainted, and then almost fainted again when she mentioned using her egg for our second child, but other than that, I was handling it pretty well. For me, at least.

I told her I was fine, not to worry, and I'd be home soon.

Again, she texted that she was on her way to meet me at Frankie's.

Wow. And she said I had trust issues. Jeez Louise, I only went out for a bike ride, like I did every other day of the week. I wasn't freaking out. And I didn't like the insinuation that I was. So in the past I hadn't handled things all that well. Okay, I had tried to sabotage my relationship with Sarah by attempting to seduce Maddie, who was not only my friend but also my brother's fiancée at the time.

I bobbed my head, understanding how bad that sounded. And it was. But did it warrant always being reminded of that every time something monumental happened in our lives?

Had her announcement shocked the hell out of me yesterday? Hell yes!

Had I fainted? Check.

Had I acted immature? Somewhat.

But had I gone over the edge? Not at all.

That was a good sign for me.

The waitress set my cinnamon roll down in front of me.

"Thank you," I said, smearing melted butter all over the top. There was nothing like a Frankie's cinnamon roll on a spring Sunday morning after a beautiful bike ride.

Why did my girlfriend—*fuck, I mean wife*—have to ruin it for me? Shit, she acted like I hadn't changed one iota.

By the time Sarah strolled into Frankie's, I was ready to give her a piece of my mind. Seriously, she had to stop treating me like a delicate flower that might go to seed each time something popped up. But then I spied Maddie, hot on Sarah's heels. They both looked blank, like something had happened. Something bad. Did someone die?

All I wanted to do was enjoy my Sunday morning. I looked down at my half-eaten roll and selfishly thought about asking them to wait until I had finished. Wasn't there a rule: no bad news on a Sunday before nine?

The two messengers sat down at the booth, and I motioned to the cheerful waitress to bring two cups of coffee.

"Righty-O. Coming right up!"

"How was your bike ride?" Sarah didn't look me in the eye; instead, she fidgeted with the drinking straw in my water glass.

"Very enjoyable. A bit crisp, but a gorgeous start to the day." I tried to maintain a happy demeanor, hoping the two doomsayers wouldn't panic about the news they had to break to me. I was trying—maybe too hard. I saw Maddie give Sarah a worried glance.

"That's nice. You'd think that after two years you'd be able to sleep in past five."

I smiled—unhappily, but doing my damnedest to be convincing. Happy as a clam. A clam that was ready to snap its shell shut and ignore whatever news they brought. Wait— was that what they were worried about?

Pull it together, Lizzie.

"So, why are you two out of bed so early on a Sunday?" Maybe if I just kept thinking or saying the word "Sunday," the happy-go-lucky feeling would stick around, no matter what.

"Peter called me," said Maddie.

Peter? My brother, and her ex-fiancé. Hey, maybe this

news wasn't about me at all. Maybe Maddie was having a bad day and she needed me. Things were looking up—for me, at least. I took a cheerful bite of my cinnamon roll and motioned for Sarah and Maddie to help themselves. Neither did. Shit! That was bad.

"What's up with Peter?"

"He wanted to let me know something, so I could tell you." Maddie leveled her gaze on me.

"Why didn't he just call me?" Ever since I had left the wedding with Maddie when she jilted him at the altar, my brother hadn't spoken to me. Not that we were close before that, but his obvious avoidance since then still irritated me. I wasn't the one who ruined his relationship; he was. He'd been having an affair, with no intention of ending it, even after Maddie found out. I was sure that in his warped mind it was all my fault. My family blamed me for everything.

Lizzie the Les-Bi-An destroys all in her diabolical homosexual path.

"Well, you know that's not going to happen." Maddie crossed her arms. "He has to talk to me. He has to play nice so my father won't ruin his career."

"My father can ruin his career as well." I said, even though I felt childish. Peter and my father were in the same business: finance. They made shitloads of money while I was content making a lot less but doing a job I loved. My mother hated that about me. She never could understand why I loved studying history. Dead people didn't pay much.

"Yeah, but your father doesn't like you." She smiled to offset her bluntness.

"Thanks, Maddie, for keeping it real. So, what's the news that has you two so worried?" I motioned to their faces with my fork.

"Worried? We aren't," Sarah said, in her "pretend everything's fine" tone.

"Uh-huh. That's why you look like I'm about to go off the deep end. Go ahead, just tell me." I mentally prepared myself for the annoying tidbit about my family, something that would make my skin crawl. To say I was the black sheep was an understatement. If I didn't look so much like my brother, I would have demanded a DNA test to prove I wasn't related to anyone in the hateful Petrie clan.

"Your mom's sick." Maddie stirred the coffee the waitress had just placed in front of her; I suspected only because it gave her something to do, since she hadn't added any sugar or cream.

"Like the flu sick?" I couldn't see the big deal. It wasn't like I was about to rush out of Frankie's to whip up a batch of chicken noodle soup for my mom—the woman I liked to call The Scotch-lady since that was the only beverage she ever consumed.

"Actually, it's a bit worse than the flu." Sarah jumped into the fire.

Worse than the flu? Well, I hated colds more than the flu for the simple fact that colds lingered for days, if not weeks. The flu made you shit your pants or puke up your guts for a few days, and then it was done. I preferred that.

"Can one of you give it to me straight?"

"Okay—" Maddie looked to Sarah for help. "She has cancer, Lizzie."

I gazed at Sarah, not comprehending. My mom was one tough broad. Nothing could kill her. Cancer and my mom didn't add up. I mean, if Death arrived on Mom's front doorstep, she'd let out a hiss that would make him tremble and tell him to crawl back to hell.

Cancer?

Cancer—and my mom?

No, simply not possible.

"Breast cancer?" I probed.

"No. Colon."

Of all the cancers, she would get colon cancer.

Jesus, Lizzie. Stop being such a heartless bitch.

This was not the time for asshole jokes.

None of us spoke. Their expressions told me it was true, but I was having a hard time digesting it.

The big C.

I was never close to Mom, that much was true; yet I wouldn't wish this on my worst enemy. Cancer didn't mess around. Before I was diagnosed with Graves' Disease, I was tested for cancer. And I was scared shitless. Seriously! I didn't intend for that to be a pun.

Fuck!

The word echoed inside my head, even though I sat mute at the table. Sarah and Maddie passed questioning looks back and forth.

Finally, I broke the silence. "Did they catch it early?"

Maddie shook her head. "I don't think so. You know your mother. Peter said she refused to go to the doctor, even though he kept encouraging her to."

"So there's no hope?" Damn it was hard to keep my voice from cracking. Why was it so hard? I wasn't close to my mother, but that didn't stop me from feeling like my whole world was crumbling down around me.

"Your father wants to have a chat with you." Maddie didn't take her eyes off her coffee. She continued to stir. Did she feel less helpless staying busy?

"Peter called you to give me the news and to have you set up a meeting with my father, is that the gist of the phone call?"

Maddie nodded.

Sarah put her hand on my arm. "Are you okay?"

I looked at her, confused. My reply sounded like it came from far away. "I don't know," was all I could say.

* * *

My father wanted to meet at a restaurant near his work, not at home. I wasn't surprised, considering I wasn't a frequent guest. I knew where they lived, of course—I grew up there—but I wasn't itching to visit, and they weren't itching to have me over for dinner; up until this point, that had worked well for all involved.

My father sat in the bar. The lights were dim, and a small candle flickered on the table, which sat between two leather chairs. Even in the gloom, I could see that he was troubled. He stared down at his bourbon, the glass containing the honey-colored liquid gripped in both hands. Dad looked old. My dad, Charles Petrie, had always given the impression of a businessman who was used to being in charge, used to being right. Now, my father looked feeble. His wrinkled three-piece suit suggested a confused man. His scarlet tie was tugged loose, and the top button of his blue silk shirt was undone. I couldn't ever remember seeing my father's tie loosened so haphazardly. I spied pink pages tucked into the side of the chair. He didn't even have the energy to read *The Financial Times* while waiting for me.

"Hello." I slipped into the leather chair opposite, feeling underdressed in jeans. I knew the establishment, but I still hadn't been able to bring myself to dress appropriately—not that the staff minded. The clientele was a mix of business people and other, more down-to-earth folk like me, family members of the professional types.

"Hello, Lizzie. Thanks for joining me this evening." Dad sat up straighter, cultivating the illusion that he was in charge.

I nodded. Was this going to be a business meeting? Item one on the agenda: your mom has cancer. Item two: what's new with you?

Dad swirled the bourbon in his glass. A waiter approached and asked if I would like anything to drink. I ordered an Earl Grey.

"If you would like a drink, I can have Matthew drive you home."

Matthew was my father's driver. About ten years ago, my mother insisted my father must have someone drive him to and from work. It was a ridiculous notion, but my father didn't put up much of a fight. Maybe he enjoyed the peaceful ride. I pictured him with a cup of coffee in the morning, rustling through *The Financial Times*, and then sipping bourbon on the evening leg while checking his emails. My father always worked. His downtime was reading financial reports. International finance never stopped; neither did Dad.

"Is it that bad?" I asked. Maybe I would take him up on the idea. I wasn't the type of person who could have one drink and be fine to drive. A whiff of alcohol made me feel tipsy.

"It's not good. Do you know anything about colon cancer?" He sounded tired, beneath the businessman composure.

I shook my head and poured milk into my tea.

"At first, the doctors weren't too alarmed. She had a colon resection—"

I cut him off. "Resection? As in removal?"

"Yes. They removed seventeen centimeters."

I turned my head to the side and let out a long breath. "I didn't know she even had surgery."

Dad looked as though he was about to say something unpleasant, but he swallowed some bourbon instead. "Peter didn't know about it at the time, either."

That was so my mother. She wouldn't want anyone to know she was sick or having surgery, let alone of the colon. I bet she was even pissed off about the word itself—"colon." Prim and proper, that was my mom. I wondered if she'd insisted on wearing one of her navy suits throughout the procedure. Imagining her in a hospital gown was … well, it was unfathomable.

"Was the surgery successful?" My voice sounded small, which made me flush, heat creeping up my neck.

"Yes." Dad took another sip of liquid courage. "And no. It's metastasized in her liver. She has Stage Four colon cancer."

"How many stages are there?" Four didn't sound great, but was it out of ten?

"Four."

I rubbed my forehead, shielding my eyes. Come on, Lizzie, don't lose it in front of him.

Him.

I didn't want to cry in front of my father—how fucked up was that?

Dad leaned all the way back in his chair and placed both arms firmly on the red leather armrests. His knuckles were fish-belly white. "I know you and your mother haven't always seen eye to eye."

Like, never.

"But I know she needs you right now." He stopped, staring over at me to ensure I was looking at him. "And I need you."

Now they wanted me to be a part of the family. It was suddenly okay to invite the lesbian back into the family fold.

Shit no! I didn't want to forget everything and play the loving, dutiful daughter.

Actually, that wasn't a fair assessment. My father spoke so rarely that I never knew whether he was bothered by the fact I was a lesbian. My mother always spoke her mind. She made it very clear that having a lesbian daughter was the worst thing that ever happened to her. My father? Well, I didn't know him at all. To this day, I couldn't tell you whether he was religious, Republican or Democrat, or anything personal about him.

"What do you need?" I couldn't stop the words from escaping my mouth.

"I've hired a nurse to take care of her at home. But your mom doesn't want the nurse to take her to and from appointments." He squirmed in his chair; it didn't become him. He was too serious a man to fidget. Clearly, Mom's illness was getting to all of us.

"She has her first appointment next week, but I'm sure she'd like to see you before then."

I didn't think my mom wanted a friendly chat. She

wanted to make sure I would toe the line, act like a doting daughter. All she ever cared about was keeping up appearances.

The last time I saw my mother, I had just learned that my father had been having affairs for most of their marriage. I felt sorry for her, briefly. After some thought, I realized she put up with it so she could be a rich man's wife and enjoy all of the glory that went with it: money, vacations, social status. She cared more about what other people thought about her than she did that the man supposed to be closest to her was a cheater. Some days, I felt sorry for her; others, angry.

Now, sitting across from my father—the cheater—I didn't know what to think. It wasn't like my parents had ever been a doting couple. I can't remember them ever acting like they were in love, or like they were even friends. It was always business in our home. Appearances mattered above everything else.

When I came out as a lesbian, my mother went into a tizzy. Before, she tolerated me somewhat. I wasn't the best daughter, but I wasn't the worst either, in her opinion. Mostly, she put up with my weaknesses, such as being shy, an animal lover, an environmentalist, and a historian. It wasn't as if she was kind to me. She was not a kind woman. But, after I came out, it was all-out warfare.

And now my father had the gall to tell me my mother needed me. I wanted to tell him to fuck off. How dare he? How dare my mother? Why couldn't Peter, the favorite, take her to appointments? Peter, the good son, the one always idolized in our family. The one who went into business, not history. The one who would settle down, marry a respectable woman, and have grandchildren my mother could brag about at the country club.

If Sarah and I had a child (or when, I guess), I had no plans to tell my parents. No way would I put my child through what they put me through. I gritted my teeth.

But now that Mom had cancer, it was supposed to be a

game changer. I would come back home. I would be the good daughter.

Fuck that.

Stage Four colon cancer. Why did this have to happen?

I wanted to scream, to throw my teacup across the room, to stomp out of the place and forget all about them. They sure hadn't ever tried to track me down just to say hi, not even when my book was published. I didn't get a phone call saying, "Congrats. We're proud of you."

Ignored.

That was all they ever did. Ignored me. Swept me under the rug.

"Would you like to order another drink?" The waiter broke the silence.

My father motioned for more bourbon. Then he shocked the hell out of me. "Would you stay for dinner? I could use the company."

I nodded and ordered a gin and tonic; then I excused myself to call Sarah and ask her to pick me up. The drive would take her more than an hour, and I figured we'd be done with dinner by then. Dad wasn't one to linger after a meal.

My father and I sat at a small table, out of view of the entrance. My mother would have shit a brick if the hostess had tried to seat us at a table where the Petrie family couldn't be seen, together. My father was different. He enjoyed the best of the best, but he liked to be out of the spotlight. I started to realize how different they were. And how much I was like my father.

We didn't chat much, and Dad barely touched his rack of lamb after it arrived.

"Are you okay to drive?" he asked as we exited the restaurant. "Matthew wouldn't mind."

"Thanks, but my w——" Shit! I almost said my wife. Most days, I forgot she was my wife, but tonight, of all nights, I'd called her my wife. "Sarah is picking me up," I rushed to cover my mistake. I had consumed two more gin and tonics over dinner, and the lights outside were starting to blur.

Dad placed a hand on my shoulder. "I always liked her. A beautiful woman. Intelligent."

I stood there, dumbfounded. Never had my father acknowledged a woman I was involved with. He'd met Sarah on a few occasions, but I didn't remember him ever speaking with her. Now he was speaking about her.

Dad put his hand out, and I shook it.

Were we sealing a business deal?

Then he walked away, to his car. Matthew held the door open, and my father disappeared into his domain. Matthew nodded at me before getting behind the wheel and pulling away from the curb. I stood on the sidewalk, near the valet stand, waiting for Sarah to pull up.

When she did, I noticed Maddie was in the car, too. She hopped out, gave me a hug, and put her hand out for my keys. "We thought it'd be easier to drive your car back tonight, instead of coming back in the morning. Where are you parked?"

"Thank you," I said, pointing to my car. Why hadn't I thought of that?

Maddie threw me a quizzical look. "Must have been an odd dinner. You okay?"

"She has Stage Four colon cancer." They were the only words I could think to say, as though no other words in the world mattered.

Maddie nodded and led me to the passenger side of Sarah's car.

"How are yo—" Sarah started, but I shot her a look that told her I didn't want to answer an unanswerable question.

Okay? Who would be okay right now?

My mother despised me, and I reciprocated; yet she had requested that I take her to all of her doctor appointments. Why? I rubbed my face with both hands, hoping that when I opened my eyes, everything would be clear. Sarah placed her hand on my knee while she waited for Maddie to pull out. I opened my eyes slowly. Clarity didn't return.

Soon, we were on I-25 heading north to our home in Fort Collins. All I wanted to do was crawl into bed. All I wanted to do was forget everything.

* * *

Sarah's alarm trilled.

I pictured her groaning and slamming her hand down to silence the alarm's shrill intrusion. She wasn't much of a morning person. She never understood why I habitually hopped out of bed early to ride. This morning, though, I wasn't on my bike. I sat at our kitchen table, nursing a lukewarm cup of tea. On the drive home last night, all I had wanted to do was crawl into bed. However, once there, I couldn't stop my mind from bouncing all over the place, rendering sleep impossible.

I decided to be useful and set about making Sarah a cup of coffee. She was still in the shower by the time it was ready, so I carried it into the bathroom and opened the shower door to say good morning. She needed more than a sip of coffee to jumpstart her brain in the morning; Sarah was usually a zombie until her second cup.

"Jesus Christ, Lizzie!" She placed a hand on her chest and sucked in a breath. "You scared the crap out of me."

"Sorry. Just thought you'd like some coffee." I raised the cup so she could see the vapors, mingling with steam from the shower, enticing her.

She shut off the water and wrapped a towel around her body, stepping out and placing a kiss on my cheek. "Thank you." She took the cup from me and gave it a greedy slurp. "I thought you were out riding."

I waved the idea away. "Couldn't sleep so I got up late. I didn't realize the time until I heard your alarm."

Her face softened, as if struck by the memory of picking me up last night, after my dinner with my estranged father. "I'm sorry. Is there anything I can do for you?"

I wanted her to stay home from work, but I knew she couldn't. Sarah hardly ever missed a day of teaching. Shaking my head, I said, "Not really."

She let her towel drop and walked toward me, hips swaying seductively. "Nothing at all?"

Sometimes, when I looked at Sarah completely naked, I had to pinch myself; this was one of those times. "You might be late," I teased.

She kissed my neck, her lips still wet from the shower. "I'll drive really fast," she whispered, pushing me backward into the bedroom.

We tumbled onto the bed.

As it turned out, to fall asleep all I needed was a roll in the hay. I vaguely remember Sarah getting up afterward, rushing around, getting ready. Before she left, Sarah flicked a strand of hair off my forehead and replaced it with a tender kiss.

A few hours later, my phone beeped. Even rubbing my eyes with the palms of my hands couldn't clear away the fogginess. When my eyes finally focused, I checked my text messages.

"*You have twenty minutes to get ready.*"

Maddie—letting me know she was playing hooky and she expected me to join her.

I grunted. All I wanted to do was to stay in bed all day. I set my phone aside, intending to ignore her. My cell beeped again.

"*I'm not kidding.*"

"Jeez, Maddie," I muttered as I pulled myself out of bed and into the shower.

She arrived five minutes early, brandishing a Starbucks chai latte.

"Thanks." I ripped the cover off and sucked in the delicious steam. "What time did Sarah call you to check on me?"

"Suspicious much, Lizzie?" Maddie's hands formed

determined triangles on her hips.

I tilted my head, waiting.

"As soon as she left. She said you didn't sleep at all last night."

"Couldn't turn my brain off."

"You finally found it, then." She smiled and arched an eyebrow.

"Oh, so funny." I took a long swallow. "Well, since you're my babysitter today, what's the plan?"

"The zoo."

"You've got to be kidding. I'm not five," I jeered.

"Have you ever been to the zoo?"

Maddie had me there, and she knew it.

"So don't knock it until you try it. Besides, once you have a kid, you'll need to know how to get there."

Kid. I'd completely forgotten about the baby Sarah wanted. Shit! How must Sarah be feeling? Overwhelmed? Or disappointed? She'd announced she wanted to get pregnant, and then, all of a sudden, Mom reenters my life with colon cancer. What rotten timing.

Would Sarah wonder whether I'd planned this somehow? Or whether I was fibbing, that none of this was real. No. The outlandish thought made me smile.

"That's the first time you've smiled at the mention of your child."

Maddie looked so impressed with herself that I didn't have the heart to confess the truth. Instead, I steered the conversation to a topic I knew she loved. "Can we grab some breakfast first? I'm ravenous."

She gave me that knowing smile of hers. "Did you two get naked earlier?"

"Maddie!" I stormed out of the room, calling for Hank, my cat, to say good-bye. Not that he cared when I came and went, as long as his food dish was full and his cat flap was open during daylight hours. But even after we moved to a quieter neighborhood, it took me weeks to trust him on his own outside.

When I returned to the kitchen, Maddie was still giggling. She and Sarah could talk about sex all day, and often did around me. Not me. Maddie told me once that Peter was the same way: he couldn't discuss it. I think I went into shock. Who in their right mind wanted to know they were as sexually repressed as their brother? Sometimes, I thought Maddie brought the subject up to distract me. This morning, it was working.

I fidgeted in the passenger seat as we traveled back to Denver to go to the "magical" zoo that was meant to take my mind off my disaster of a life.

"It's okay, you know," Maddie said.

We hadn't spoken for miles, so I had no clue what she was talking about. "What is?" I placed my empty chai cup in the holder.

"Feeling conflicted, about your mom?" She tapped the steering wheel in tune with the radio.

I stared out the window. I did my best to concentrate on some cows coming into view in the distance. If I didn't, tears would fall. "I don't know what to think or feel. All night I wondered why I couldn't feel sad. I mean, I am sad, but I'm not devastated." I leaned against the headrest. "I'm such a crappy person."

"That's true, but not about this, at least." Maddie's voice gave no indication whether she was teasing or not. She could be a difficult person to read. She had a knack for saying things that, in her Southern tone, could mean anything.

I opened one eye and saw her smile. "Thanks."

"Let's face it, Lizzie. Your mom would never win any Best Mom awards. You haven't spoken to her since the wedding, and now, all of a sudden, she wants you to be there for her. It's fucked up."

"So you wouldn't do it?" I felt hopeful.

"Oh, no. I'd take her." Maddie took her eyes of the road briefly to make eye contact. "No matter what, she's your mom. Maybe this experience will be good for you two. If you turned your back now, I know you'd let it tear you up inside."

"Why is it I only feel two emotions around my mother: guilt and anger?"

"Families. Gotta love them."

"I need to pee."

Maddie cocked her head, insinuating she knew I was using it as a diversionary tactic. To my surprise, she didn't object. We pulled off at the next gas station. I hid in the bathroom for several minutes, feeling silly. A gas station bathroom wasn't the best place to gather one's thoughts. Before I was ready, I stepped outside.

The sun blazed above. I couldn't help but feel a tad excited about the zoo. The Petrie family didn't do the regular family things: zoos, soccer games, bowling, movies. Maybe having a child with Sarah would give me the chance to experience the things I'd missed out on as a child. Goodness knows Maddie and Sarah wouldn't let me miss out on those types of events. Was I ready to spend every weekend doing something new? Would Sarah insist on taking tons of photos and then spending hours scrapbooking, like she had after our wedding? I had only just recovered from all of that insanity.

Maddie honked the horn and stuck her head out the window. "Move it, or lose it."

I laughed. Was she serious? I was pretty sure Maddie wouldn't actually mow me down in the gas station parking lot? But knowing her, I decided not to press my luck.

* * *

Turned out, otters were the most adorable creatures I'd ever seen. I stood outside, watching one little guy float on his back and slam a rock into a clam. I couldn't get enough. Two more chased each other in the water. Maybe this was why Mom had never taken me to the zoo: it'd prove to her that I was completely hopeless. For Mom, animals weren't cute; they were a nuisance. I wouldn't be surprised if she signed a petition to do away with all animals and zoos.

Maddie stood off to the side, talking on the phone with one of her clients. It always amazed me that she could be away from the office and still manage to get work done. If I didn't lock myself in my office at home, I wouldn't accomplish a thing.

My latest research project—the role young women played in the Third Reich—was fascinating, but I still often found myself staring out of my window instead of pouring over my books, researching, or writing. My publisher had pitched the idea after I completed my book on the Hitler Youth, the Nazi version of the Boy Scouts. For the most part, women, especially young women, had been excluded from the history books during that time period.

Oh God, if my mother found out about my new project, she'd be irate. "So now you're a feminist, too! It's not bad enough you're a lesbian. You have to be the voice of Nazi women. Nazis! What will they say at the club?" The opinion of the ladies at the club was all that mattered to my mom. Did they know she was sick? Let them take care of her.

I was so busy having this mental discussion that I jumped when Maddie tugged on my shirt.

"Come on, let's check out the baby animals."

When we exited the zoo, I asked Maddie if we could stop at the Tattered Cover bookstore in Cherry Creek. I had spent many a day there when I was in high school. The store was massive, with so many wonderful nooks and crannies that a book lover could get lost there and completely forget about the outside world. On most visits, I went straight for the history or audiobook section. Today, I had a different mission: parenting books.

If nothing else, today had proved I was clueless. Shit! I hadn't even been to a zoo before! At thirty years of age I was, until very recently, a zoo virgin. My child deserved better. I considered asking Sarah to go bowling later.

Maddie appeared around the corner, a stack of books

piled in her arms—mostly chick lit and romance. All of the covers were either pink or purple. "I've been looking everywhere for you, but never thought to check here." She eyed the shelves, but said nothing.

"Research," I said, ashamed I couldn't admit the whole truth. I was terrified I'd be a shitty parent—just like mine. "Are you ready? Sarah should be home in a couple of hours."

Maddie nodded and followed me to the registers.

"You busy tonight?" I asked Maddie as she pulled the car off the highway, onto Harmony Road in Fort Collins.

"Why? What do you have in mind?"

"I thought the three of us could go bowling." I said it as if we went bowling all the time.

"Bowling?" she chortled. "Oh, this I have to see." Before I could change my mind, Maddie hit a button on the steering wheel and the phone started dialing. Sarah's number on speed dial, I guessed. Maddie always made or answered hands-free phone calls to and from clients while driving. "Sarah, Lizzie wants to take us bowling."

"Are you in the car?" Sarah replied. I could sense a smile in her tone.

"Yes, so I can hear everything you say," I said. "Go ahead and laugh. Maddie already did."

I heard muffled laughter. "I'm not laughi—" she couldn't get out the rest of the word.

"Shall we meet you at home?" Maddie said.

"Ye—" More giggling.

This was going to be a long night. Why had I thought it was a good idea? Could I really squeeze a whole childhood into one day?

CHAPTER THREE

Several days later, I pulled my new SUV into my parents' driveway. Several months back, Sarah had insisted we needed the car. I realized this was another clue I had missed.

It was eleven in the morning, and I knew my father would be at work. Mom's condition wouldn't change his work routine, not one bit. More than likely, Peter would continue his seventy-hour working weeks as well.

I had tried calling Peter to talk about Mom. He finally responded to a text and told me she'd more than likely be home on Tuesday. More than likely. She had cancer. Did Peter think she was out on the town, shopping?

I sat in the car, deciding what my next move should be. I felt chickenshit. My instincts screamed at me to put the car in reverse. To tell everyone that I had stopped by but Mom was out. Simple as that. I tried, really tried, to be there for her, I could say, appeasing the guilt. Maybe I could even actually convince myself that I had tried.

My hand started to pull back on the gearshift. All I had to do was pull it back to R. My nanny used to say, "R is for rocket." As a kid, I spent more time in cars with Annie than I did with my own mother. It was probably safer that way, since my mother was hardly ever sober.

Why should I be there for her?

Because she has cancer, you douchebag.

I put the car in park again and opened the door.

Just get out of the car. Baby steps, Lizzie. Baby steps.

Goddammit, just go and ring the front doorbell. You're better than this. Just fucking do it.

I trudged up the front steps and raised my hand to press the bell, suddenly realizing how ridiculous it was that I had to ring the bell to enter my parents' home. I grew up here. Why didn't I just walk in?

The thought angered me. I turned around and started back to the car, stopping abruptly when I heard the front door open.

"What'd you want?" My mother bellowed.

Shit! Now I looked like a coward: the exact image she always had of me.

I turned around slowly, snapping my mouth shut so I wouldn't look completely asinine. "I just—"

"Oh, it's you. I thought … well, it doesn't matter." She waved an arm limply, erasing her thought.

"Hi. I just stopped by to say, well … hi." I shifted nervously from one foot to the other.

She looked twenty years older than the last time I had seen her. She wasn't wearing one of her usual navy pinstripe power suits; instead, she wore royal-blue silk pajamas and a matching robe. I couldn't remember ever seeing my mom in pajamas. I was under the illusion that she slept in her skirt and crisp white shirt.

"Do you want to come in, or do you want to continue standing outside, looking foolish?"

Mom still had a way with words.

Keep it together, Lizzie. Remember she has cancer, for Christ's sake.

"Thanks. You look good, Mom."

"I hope you're a better historian than you are a liar," she scoffed.

I gawked at her. She turned her back on me, and led me

to the family room. I hadn't been in the Petrie family home for years. Besides a new coat of paint on the walls, everything looked the same. An overstuffed burgundy leather couch with matching chairs took up most of the front room. Off to the side of the fireplace stood a small bar, home to several crystal decanters. The coffee table was glass, and spotless. A book sat on the floor by one of the leather chairs, and I was shocked when my mom nestled down into the chair. Was she reading a book? I knew she could read, but I couldn't remember her ever reading much. I glanced at the cover and almost fell over. It was a copy of my book.

"Would you mind making me a cup of tea?" It was a question, but her face told me it was also a demand.

"Uh, sure." I needed to be alone for a moment or two, to pull myself together. My mom had not only purchased a copy of my book (and not many people had), but she was also actually reading it! Why? A book on the Hitler Youth wasn't exactly uplifting material for a person dealing with chemo treatments. Then again, maybe she liked depressing, survival-of-the-fittest shit at the moment. It did fit her acerbic personality.

I placed the teapot, cups, creamer, and sugar bowl on a silver tray and carried it into the front room. "I wasn't sure if you wanted milk and sugar."

My mom nodded. "Yes."

I fixed her a cup and handed it to her, making sure I didn't forget the saucer.

She didn't say thanks, just sank further into her chair. It engulfed her, diminishing her meanness. I glanced down at the floor and saw that the book was now out of view. Had she shoved it under the chair or tossed it in the trashcan off to the right of the room?

"Peter called," I started, not knowing where to go with that conversation.

"I assumed. It's not like you to stop by." She sipped her tea without flinching, even though I knew it was blistering hot.

I poured more milk into my cup.

"Oh, you made yourself a cup."

I couldn't tell from her expression whether she had meant to say that out loud, or whether she even noticed she had verbalized the thought. How dare I enjoy a cup of tea? My mother never wanted me to have an easy life. She despised that my father had set up a trust fund for me. She made it perfectly clear that I was an undeserving disappointment—a humongous stain on her happiness. And now I had waltzed into her home and helped myself to her tea supply. Lizzie the Les-Bi-An strikes again.

I didn't respond. I was trying to be the bigger person. "How are you feeling?" I asked eventually.

She sighed, nostrils flared. "How do you think I'm feeling?"

Mental note: don't ask The Scotch-lady how she feels.

"I—"

"Don't pretend you care. I'm sure Peter told you to visit, to say your peace so you wouldn't have to live with guilt and all that hippie crapola Oprah preaches about. So you did. Don't expect me to be grateful. I don't need pity. Not Peter's. Not yours. No one's."

Hippie crapola. What decade was this? And didn't Oprah retire or something?

I ignored her tirade. "Will you have someone looking after you ... when you start your treatments?" I already knew the answer, but I couldn't think of anything else to say.

"Yes. Your father hired a nurse. That's who I thought was at the door." Her voice dripped with revulsion at "father."

I could tell the war hadn't ended. My parents didn't scream or shout at each other, but they did things to each other that hurt like hell—like not being there when your spouse was undergoing chemotherapy.

I shuddered at the thought of living my life with

someone I hated. Neither of them ever mentioned the D-word. Divorce didn't happen to nice families like ours. My mom's definition of a nice family was a wealthy family.

Mom had no siblings to help her out. I was sure Peter would stop by every evening, but he wouldn't actually do anything to help. My father and my brother preferred to hire help to deal with things they didn't want to do personally. But Mom wasn't a chore—or, at least, she shouldn't be. Regardless, being around her was hell. I wasn't about to offer my time to take care of her. Maybe I was just as bad as the other two.

"Is there anything I can do for you?" I asked.

"Yes, I would like some books to read. The one I'm reading now—it's so dry." She turned dry into a two-syllable word.

I didn't flinch. "Okay, what type of books?"

"Whatever's popular these days." Her eyes dulled. She'd already lost interest. I think she only mentioned the idea so she could take a dig at me.

"Anything else. Food?" I almost asked if she wanted me to pick up some scotch, her favorite drink. Actually, until today, I don't think I'd ever seen The Scotch-lady drink anything else.

"No. We can afford to have our groceries delivered," she barked.

Another dig. I could afford it as well, but we opted to do our own shopping.

"Sure." I guzzled my tea. "I'll be back soon." I needed to get out of there before I lost my temper.

"Wait." She shifted in her chair. I could tell she was having a hard time keeping her eyes open. "Why don't you bring the books by tomorrow, or the next day?"

Shit. I had hoped this would be a one-time thing. Surely my father didn't expect me to chauffeur Mom to all of her appointments and spend "quality" time with her.

The Scotch-lady's eyes flickered with an idea. "Actually,

next Wednesday. Then you can take me to my appointment."

Holy shit. Did she just ask me to take her to her appointment? From her demeanor earlier, I assumed it was my father's idea for me to take Mom to and from her appointments and that she wasn't on board or didn't know about the plan. But she was on board.

Jesus, I wasn't ready for this. I just wanted to buy the bitter woman some books, appease my guilt, not be her nurse, or her daughter.

"Sure, I can do that. What time?"

"Nine." She forced her eyes open. "So be here at eight, since you're always late." Mom closed her eyelids once more, and I knew sleep would overtake her soon.

I didn't bother saying good-bye; it would be superfluous. I had been dismissed, as if I were a member of the household staff, but not before I was given my orders: buy books and take Mom to her appointment.

My one problem—well the most pressing concern, at least—was finding books my mom would like to read. I felt as though it was a test. Most of the books I read were about Nazis, but Mom made it clear that not only was my book a letdown, but also that my specialty was too dull for her.

I needed help.

Ethan and Sarah were English teachers. I shot Ethan a text asking if we could have a coffee date at Barnes & Noble in Fort Collins. His town, Loveland, had no bookstore, and Fort Collins was only a ten-minute drive from his house.

What types of books would a crabby woman with colon cancer read? I suddenly realized I didn't know. I did not know the first thing about my mother. If Sarah asked me to buy her a book, I would know exactly what she'd like: sappy, something with a pink cover. But my mom? I had no fucking clue.

* * *

My SOS worked. On Saturday afternoon, Sarah and I

sauntered into the coffee section in Barnes & Noble on College Avenue and found Ethan, Lisa, their daughter, and Maddie waiting for us. Ethan and Maddie were embroiled in a comical conversation, and Maddie was trying not to choke on her latte. Ethan gently patted her back, doing his best not to pee his pants over her antics. The woman didn't suffer quietly.

"Anyone need a refill?" I asked, gesturing to their coffee cups before slipping into the line to order drinks for Sarah and myself.

Usually, I couldn't stand waiting in line, but I didn't want this one to end. Once it did, I would have to start searching for books for a woman who had given birth to me—that was pretty much all I knew about her. I felt like I was meeting my biological mother for the first time. It wasn't far from the truth. Mom didn't give me away at birth, but she did basically give up on me shortly thereafter.

Thirty years later, she was dying. It took her getting cancer for me to recognize that I didn't know my own mother, and that I might want to learn more about her.

I slumped down into a chair, ready to face the book inquisition.

"So, give it to me straight, how screwed am I?" I stared at each blank face. The only one not paying attention was Lisa. She was busy entertaining Casey, who was three-going-on-sixteen. The child wore a princess outfit including sparkling gloves, a tiara, a boa, and a wand. God, I really hoped Sarah and I had a son. How would I handle my kid dressing up like a Disney princess in the middle of spring? On Halloween, I could live with it, maybe.

"What did you tell me once"—Ethan knitted his brow and his Coke-bottle glasses hitched up—"your mother has no qualms about ripping the heads off kittens."

"Yeah, I'm toast." I slurped my chai.

"Now hold on you two. Let's not get all dramatic. I think it's wonderful that your mom wants you there." Sarah plastered a supportive grin on her face. It was phony as hell, but I appreciated the effort.

Maddie looked away and started humming the theme song from *Jaws*, making Ethan giggle uncontrollably. Maddie laughed so hard she had to excuse herself and step outside. I watched her wiggle her arms frantically and wipe the tears from her face. Before returning, she checked her reflection in the glass door to ensure her mascara wasn't smudged.

Casey climbed into my lap, as if it was the most natural thing in the world. "Do you like Ariel?"

"Ariel?" I asked unsure if that was a real word.

"*The Little Mermaid,*" explained Ethan.

"The what? The statue in Copenhagen?" Why did they name her Ariel? It didn't sound Danish to me.

"Seriously, Lizzie. You're such a dork sometimes," Ethan shook his head in amazement and smoothed the top of his perfectly styled hair.

"Ariel—from the Disney movie." Lisa pushed a book into my hand and spoke slowly, as if I was the three-year-old here.

Sarah observed me closely, concern etched on her face. I was sure she was realizing I needed some major education about raising kids. Would she come home tomorrow with a bunch of Disney movies for me to watch?

"Read to me," Casey demanded as she snuggled against my chest.

Ethan raised his eyebrows over the rim of his glasses.

"That's a great idea." Maddie obviously saw it as an opportunity. "You read to Casey, and the rest of us will look for books for your mom. I'm pretty sure she doesn't want anything that would catch your eye."

Everyone but Lisa stood. Ethan gave an almost imperceptible shake of his head, and Lisa reluctantly left her child with me: the person who didn't know Ariel.

Casey tapped the book, and I started to read it aloud, although as quietly as possible. I didn't want the entire store to think I was a loon. Two minutes in, Casey hopped off my lap and began to wander in the store. I followed, uneasy about her wobbly legs, eyeballing strangers who might be child-stealing kooks. People smiled as she weaved in and out of the crowd. I gave each one a curt nod and then got back to my guard duty. There was no rhyme or reason to her meanderings.

Spying the children's section in the back, I swooped Casey up in my arms. "Let's go play."

"Yippee!" she shouted, tapping me on top of the head with her magic wand and giggling madly. I wanted to throttle Ethan for saddling me with his demented fairytale kid.

On the way, a book caught my eye. I grabbed it off the shelf.

I had never set foot into the children's section before. Maybe I had when I was a kid, but I had no memories of ever being there.

The place was a disaster. A cursory glance revealed seven kids running amok. Two of them crashed into each other—hard. But not hard enough for either of them to start crying, I noticed. Then I noticed they had light sabers, but they weren't using them Luke Skywalker style. Instead, they were jousting like medieval knights. One of the knights noticed Casey in my arms.

"The princess is here!" Both of the boys bowed dramatically.

Casey clapped her gloved hands together and somehow managed to wiggle magically out of my arms.

"The enemy, your highness, is attacking!" said one little boy—I mean "knight." He raised his light saber and shouted, "Charge."

The other boy followed suit. Casey squealed in delight.

Seconds later, she was distracted by a massive dollhouse, leaving the two knights, who didn't even notice that their highness had forgotten about them, to fight it out. They were already trying to overthrow another boy, who was hiding behind a beanbag.

The scene was chaos. I was certain I had never acted like

these buffoons a day in my life. Did they have any decorum? And their parents, where were they? All I could see were employees doing their best to tidy up after each wave of children blew through like a tsunami. To their credit, the employees didn't look mad. I would be grabbing kids by their ears and throwing them out of the kids' section—*wait a minute, Lizzie. You can't throw a kid out of the kids' section.*

What was wrong with me? Sighing, I sat down on a miniature chair next to Casey.

"Would you like a cup of tea?" She'd now forgotten all about the dollhouse in favor of a tea set perched on the table in front of her.

"Uh, sure."

Her caramel eyes glowed as she pretended to pour me a cup. "Sugar?"

I nodded.

She prepared her own cup and sat down at the undersized table. The chair suited Casey, was designed for her even, but my knees jutted up above the table. I felt like an ogre.

"We went hiking this morning. Do you know what hiking is?" Casey tilted her little head, curious.

"Um, yeah sure, it's when … " Why in the world couldn't I answer a simple question? I hiked all the time. It wasn't a foreign concept to me.

"It's when you walk on dirt," she stated matter-of-factly.

I sat there, astounded. What a simple definition. Kids really got to the heart of the matter. *Walking on dirt.* I chuckled, and raised my tiny cup of pretend tea to my mouth.

"Next week, we're going to my grandparents." Casey was a chatty kid.

"That's nice. Do you like your grandparents?" I had no clue what else to say.

"I'm going to puke in a bucket!" she shouted with glee.

I looked around for a bucket. "Do you feel okay?"

"In the car. I'm going to puke in a bucket!" Again,

Ethan's daughter looked thrilled with the idea of puking in the bucket.

"She gets car sick." Ethan sat down at the table with us, grinning at the sight of me sitting at a kid's table and enjoying a cup of tea with his daughter.

"May I?" I motioned to the teapot.

"Yes, please." He ruffled the top of Casey's head, beaming at his princess.

I pretended to pour him a cup. "One lump or two?" I held out the tiny sugar bowl.

Casey giggled.

"Two, Miss Lizzie."

Casey sniggered some more. I had to admit it was catching. Trying my best not to join in, I bit my lower lip.

Ethan raised the cup and feigned burning his tongue.

"You're silly, Daddy." Casey was out of her seat like a shot. The knights were back, fighting for her honor once again.

"How's the book hunt?" I queried as I fished in my messenger bag for my bottled water.

"Oh, I think you'll be impressed by the stack. Maddie keeps trying to sneak in erotica, but Sarah is dealing with her."

"Who sent you: my wife or yours?" I crossed my arms. I knew he was checking up on me, not on Casey.

"Mine."

I raised an eyebrow.

"Okay, they both sent me. They were worried." He flicked the pages of the book sitting in front of me on the table. "I don't know why." He grinned.

I glanced at the cover of the book: *Mein Kampf*.

"Not many people sit in the children's section reading Hitler's manifesto." He suppressed a chuckle by tugging on one corner of his expertly manicured moustache.

"I saw it on the way in, and I remembered I needed to check something."

"A *Mein Kampf* emergency?" His expression was pure

amusement.

"Very funny, wise guy. Sarah made me get rid of my copy, so this seemed like a good time." I shrugged.

He let out a loud guffaw. "You really are a piece of work. Just be careful. Don't get arrested."

"Hardy har har. By the way, she's kinda funny." I motioned to Casey.

He rolled his eyes. "Wow, that was charming."

"No, I mean it. Did you know that hiking is walking on dirt? She asked me to define it and I couldn't, but she had the definition without even thinking about it."

"Kids are like that. They see things how they really are." He smiled at his daughter, who was sprinkling pretend fairy dust over the knights. "It's a shame we lose that."

"I'm not sure I ever had that."

He smiled wryly. "You? Probably not."

"I'm not sure I can do this," I warbled. "Since all of you abandoned me, I've been a nervous wreck, afraid I'd break your child or something."

Ethan placed a hand on mine. "Sure you can. Just don't think about it. If you overthink it, you'll drive yourself crazy. It'll be the best thing you've ever done. Trust me, Lizzie. And if you don't trust me, trust Sarah. That woman loves you more than you deserve."

I couldn't help but laugh. "Thanks, buddy."

"Just keeping it real for ya."

A boy dressed as Spiderman came crashing into the kids' section, running full speed before throwing himself against the wall.

I was too stunned to move or speak. No one in the room reacted. The other kids ignored him. His parents, or the people I assumed were his parents, gazed around the section and then turned to leave their insane child with all of the other innocent children, and me.

The parents paused and waved to Ethan, who gave a friendly wave back.

"Do you know them?" I whispered.

"Yes. Why are you whispering?"

"I sure hope that doesn't happen to our kid," I whispered again.

"What?" He jutted his chin out, waiting for my answer.

"You know." I fidgeted on the small chair and nearly fell out. "Having a *special* child."

Ethan burst into a fit of laughter. "Nate isn't special. He's just a boy."

"Who thinks he can scale a wall like Spiderman! Did you see the way he threw himself at the wall and then bounced back three feet? No normal person would do such a thing."

Ethan shot me a serious look. "What about Casey, do you think she's special?"

"What? No! Why?" My voice cracked more than I cared to admit.

"She's dressed as a princess."

"Uh … that." I gasped for air.

"Lizzie, calm down. I was just giving you shit." He smiled, relieving my stress a little. "Kids are kids. You can't explain what or why they do things. But you need to loosen up."

I glanced over at Casey. She was chasing Spiderman, having the time of her life. I just didn't get it.

By the time we left the store, I had eight books for Mom. Maddie tried to sneak in Fannie Flagg's *Fried Green Tomatoes at the Whistle Stop Café* at the last moment, but Sarah was watching her hawkishly. As the cashier rang up the books, I saw *Tipping the Velvet* fall into the bag and gave Maddie the evil eye.

"It's for me," Sarah explained.

I assumed the lesbian parenting books were also for her. I hadn't shown Sarah the books I bought the day Maddie took me to the zoo.

I better make sure none of those accidentally slip into my mom's pile. I'd never hear the end of that. I could hear her now, "Oh great, Les-Bi-Ans raising a child. Just what the world needs—more gays."

* * *

After Barnes & Noble, Sarah had plans with her mother, so I opted to go for a bike ride. My legs, however, weren't into it, or maybe my mind wasn't. After five miles, I turned around and headed for home. I plopped down on the sofa, flipped open my laptop, and picked up my cup of Earl Grey.

For some reason, the image of Casey in her princess outfit popped into my mind. Who did she say she was? Ariel.

I googled Ariel.

Being a nerd, I read some articles on *The Little Mermaid.* Turned out Ariel was one of Disney's most iconic characters, based on a Hans Christian Andersen fairytale, and I didn't have a fucking clue. How could I consider becoming a parent if I didn't know Ariel? Shouldn't I know that? God, I was going to be the worst parent ever.

At least I'd recognized Spiderman, although I still couldn't believe the way that little boy had thrown himself into the wall. How did he think that'd turn out? Could the child be so clueless that he actually thought he could scale a wall like Spiderman? Were boys really that stupid?

Hank jumped into my lap and swatted at Ariel on my laptop screen. Purring, he started to rub up against her. Shit! Even my cat knew more about Disney princesses than I did.

"That's it, Hank, we're going to watch *The Little Mermaid.*" I streamed the movie from Netflix. If everyone else on the planet knew about this chick, so would I.

I paused the movie during the opening credits. If I was going to watch one of the most iconic Disney characters of all time, I wanted to be in the right mood. I zapped some popcorn in the microwave, grabbed a bag of M&Ms from the pantry, and settled down in front of our new sixty-inch HD TV, which Sarah had insisted we buy last week. Sixty inches! If you'd asked me before last week whether we needed such a large TV, I would have laughed in your face. But after one day, I was hooked. Usually, I read at night while Sarah watched TV or graded papers. But this week we had settled down on the couch to watch movie after movie. And Netflix—what a brilliant idea. Thank God I didn't have this TV and Netflix when I was in grad school, or I wouldn't have finished my program.

A thought struck me. Did Sarah think I'd have the time or inclination to take care of the baby while she was working? My heart started to flutter. I felt all the blood drain out of my face.

Get a hold of yourself!

Closing my eyes, I counted to ten like my therapist had taught me. I calmed myself down.

Then I hit play and lost myself in the movie.

"Are you watching *The Little Mermaid*?"

"Shit!" Sarah's voice scared the bejesus out of me. I placed a hand on my heart. "Are you trying to kill me?"

"I'm sorry, I didn't mean to startle you." She laughed over my antics, as though I was being playful. I wasn't. If I had heard her coming in, I'd have turned the damn movie off. Now I'd never hear the end of it.

"Jeez, you could have knocked or something."

She shook her head disapprovingly. "Why would I knock to enter my own home?"

"To give me some warning."

"Why, do you plan on having an affair?"

The word "affair" hung in the air. Neither one of us knew how to handle the situation.

Finally, I joked, "No, but when I'm watching crap TV I would like some notice so I can shut it off before you arrive."

"*The Little Mermaid* is not crap!" Sarah crossed her arms, ready for battle.

"Well, it's not good for kids. Do you know the chef dude says *merde*? That's *shit* in French. How can parents let their kids watch this trash?" I felt silly saying it. Of course Sarah knew; she was fluent in French, after all. She was constantly dragging me to Denver, to her favorite theater, to see foreign films. The theater was fancy, serving cocktails and scrumptious desserts, so I didn't complain too much.

I refused to admit that I actually thought *The Little Mermaid* was pretty darn cute for a cartoon, let alone that I was on my second viewing. Next time I saw Casey, I planned to give her a run for her money. I'd show her who was an expert on *The Little Mermaid*.

Sarah motioned for me to raise my legs so she could sit down on the couch. "Lizzie, has anyone ever told you to lighten up."

"Not in the past five minutes."

"I can't believe you don't love this movie. I remember seeing it when I was a kid."

"Have you seen it since then? I bet you don't like it now."

Okay, how shameless was I? I didn't want to admit I had wanted to watch it again, so I concocted this plan. Pitiful!

"I bet I do!" She tapped my legs playfully.

"Bet you don't." Was I pushing too hard?

"Well then, go make more popcorn so I can prove you wrong."

As soon as I stepped out of view, I gave myself a high five. Instead of making popcorn, I decided to put out some cheese, chorizo, and crackers on a plate, and then I uncorked a bottle of wine. I hummed as I prepared the food, which wasn't like me one bit. I wasn't sure where the inspiration came from.

"Liar!"

I looked up to find Sarah propped against the kitchen doorframe. "What? I'm sorry. I thought this would be better than just popcorn."

"Not that." She sauntered over to the platter I had prepared and snagged a piece of chorizo. After popping it into her mouth and chewing, she said, "This looks good."

"Then why did you shout *liar*?"

"You were humming the song, 'Under the Sea.'"

"I was not," I lied with as much conviction as I could muster.

"Yes. You. Were." The look of satisfaction on her face annoyed the hell of out me.

"I don't even know what you're talking about." I whisked past her with the snacks and wine. Glancing back over my shoulder, I asked, "Can you bring the wineglasses, please?"

Sarah strode into the room after me, carrying the new wineglasses she and her mom had picked out at Pier One. "You can lie to yourself, but you can't lie to me."

I rolled my eyes. "Whatever. Can we watch this lame movie yet, or do you want to continue your jibber-jabber?"

There was no way I was going to confess that I liked the movie. No way in hell.

CHAPTER FOUR

Wednesday morning arrived much faster than I expected. I hopped out of bed at five, anxious to get going so I wouldn't be late to pick Mom up for her appointment.

I was brushing my teeth in the bathroom when Sarah slipped her arms around my waist. "You going to be okay today?"

I shrugged.

She rose on her tippy toes and kissed the back of my head. Then she turned and stepped into the shower.

Mom had told me to be at her house by eight, but I was in her neighborhood by seven. Not wanting to disturb her, I stopped at Starbucks to kill time. I fidgeted at a table, one hand nursing a chai latte and the other shakily holding open a book—an account of a young Englishwoman living under Nazi tyranny. My eyes kept darting back to paragraphs before, my brain unable to wrap itself around the words. Every few seconds, I peeked at my watch. I wanted to ensure I wasn't late, but I also secretly kept hoping time had magically stopped.

Chemo.

I pondered over the word. Just the thought of it made me shit my pants. I couldn't imagine what my mother was going through.

At 7:55 a.m., I rang the doorbell. As I waited, I straightened my shirt and swore at myself for being stupid enough to wear jeans. I could just hear my mother: *Jeans, Elizabeth? I'm dying and you wear jeans.*

The door swung open, and my neck cracked a little as I did a double take. My father held the door open for me. Since when did he go to work this late?

"Morning," he huffed, motioning me inside.

"Good morning," I mumbled, as he shut the door behind me.

The mood in the house was chilling. Maybe if we had been a closer family, it wouldn't be so tense, but I doubted it. Nothing in life prepared anyone for this.

My mother was perched on the leather sofa. One of her navy blue skirts had been paired with a starched white blouse and matching navy blazer. Her purse sat on her lap.

"Lizzie's here," my father announced—needlessly, as I was standing in plain view.

My mother opened her mouth and then snapped it shut, resembling one of those turtles you see on a nature documentary, with her wrinkled neck, thin lips, and beady eyes always on the lookout for prey.

"How you feeling?" I asked. She looked as scared as I felt. The last time I asked her that question, Mom had nearly bitten my head off, yet I couldn't think of anything else to say.

"Fine."

I lifted the bag of books. "I got you some books."

"Good. Set them by my chair," she commanded. She didn't bother saying thanks, but this time I didn't really care.

"You ready to go?" she asked.

I wanted to ask her the same thing—not in the same way, though. I meant mentally.

"Call me when you're done," my father instructed, directing his statement to me, not her. "The nurse will be here when you get back."

I nodded. He studied Mom for a split second before

retreating to the safety of his chauffeured car, his mountain of work. I wanted to shout at him. Coward!

When we arrived for the appointment I braced myself for the sterile environment beyond the door. I wasn't sure what I expected, but I didn't think the entrance would scream welcome, yet it did. A floral arrangement was the first thing that caught my eye. Colorful prints adorning the walls gave the impression this would be a cool place to have a cup of joe and catch up with friends. I hated the place immediately. The attempt to be overly cheerful was an insult to reality. People didn't come here to have coffee. They came in hope of cheating death.

My mother strode to the front desk like a cavalry officer riding into battle: full of confidence and bravado. I admired the front she was putting on.

The nurse handed her some paperwork to complete; Mom handed it straight to me. We took a seat opposite an older woman wearing a headscarf.

Jesus! I don't need to see that!

Mom's expression suggested she felt the same. She nodded at the woman, but didn't speak.

"Your first time?" the woman asked her.

"What?"

"Is this your first appointment? I can tell. I've been around for a while." The woman smiled, her expression supportive under drawn-on eyebrows. How she managed that was beyond me.

"Yes." My mother's tone was cool. She was never one for chitchat.

The woman eyed me. "It's wonderful that you're here for her."

I nodded, not knowing what to say. It was obvious she didn't have anyone, or maybe the person tired of the appointments. *How long does it take,* I wondered, *until a patient's hair falls out?*

"I need your insurance card," I told Mom, motioning

toward the intake form.

When she pulled out the card, I saw that her hand was shaking, her eyes averted. I didn't say or do anything to reassure her. Knowing Mom, that wasn't what she wanted anyway. Being human wasn't her thing.

Several minutes later, I returned the forms to the woman at the front desk. A nurse appeared in the waiting room, glancing at her clipboard and calling my mother's name. Both of us sat there, frozen. Finally, I stood and put out my hand to Mom. I half expected her to swat it away; she didn't.

It was icicle cold.

"I'll be here when you're done."

She acknowledged me with a slight tilt of her head and then strode off briskly, once again a cavalry officer.

I pulled out my book. Words blurred the page. That was when I noticed that my eyes were filled with tears. I dabbed at them casually and wiped my cheek on my shoulder. I needed to hold it together. My mom needed me to be strong.

A table offering tea and coffee sat to one side of the room. I poured myself a tea and wandered back to my chair, opening my book, pretending to read for I don't know how long until the door that led to the back opened and the nurse ushered Mom out.

"Here she is," the nurse announced, as if my mother was a child who'd just had her teeth cleaned for the first time.

"Is there anything I need to do?" Mom asked her, in a not-so-confident tone.

"Nope. You're all set. We'll see you in a couple of days."

We drove home in silence.

"I'll see you in two days," she informed me when I pulled into her driveway. Without another word, she stepped out of the car. Her nurse opened the front door of the house.

Just like that, I was dismissed. Dad's assistant took my message to let him know that Mom was back home and that everything went well. Actually, I wasn't sure what had happened, let alone whether it went according to plan. Mom left me in the dark.

I arrived back in Fort Collins before noon, feeling like I just biked one hundred miles. I sat in my SUV, unable to open the door, let alone move my arms or legs. I put the car in park. I left the seatbelt on. I stared at my driveway. I felt numb. Numb.

* * *

By the time Sarah walked in the front door, I was in much better shape, even if I'm pretty sure my splotchy cheeks and puffy eyes screamed, "I've been crying!"

My conflicting emotions confused and baffled me. Why was I was feeling overwhelmed, confused, sad, angry, and alone when Mom and I were never even close. Peter was much closer to her, even if not involved in actually taking care of her. My brother never could face reality. He was always too busy putting on a show, one that assured everyone how successful he was. I doubted it had ever occurred to him that no one cared. *People care about actions, Peter, not impressions.*

Ironically, my mother, if she didn't have cancer, would have been one of the few people impressed by the way Peter was handling things.

"How'd it go?" Sarah set her bag down. Papers brimmed out of the top, and I knew she had a full night of grading to do.

"Um, it was … surreal. I don't really know how to describe it," I said in barely more than a whisper.

"Did she get sick?" Sarah sat down next to me on the couch and rubbed my back.

I shrugged. "Not sure. She only let me take her to the appointment. When we got back to the house, she didn't even let me get out of the car to help her up the stairs. It was like I'm only good enough to take her to the hospital, or she wanted the staff members to know her daughter cared enough to take her, which implies she was a good mother. Why couldn't she just pay someone to act like her daughter and leave me out of it?"

Sarah sighed. She had never let on to me, but deep down I think she was worried about this turn of events, worried I would let Mom take advantage of me in the hope of finally earning maternal love. I knew I was worried about that as well. Why, at the age of thirty, was I still desperate for acceptance? Given that I had let my childhood memories interfere with my relationship with Sarah in the past, I admired her ability to support me silently, without giving voice to her concerns. Perhaps she sensed I had enough on my plate.

"If she's anything like you, she didn't want to show you that she's vulnerable. Give her time, Lizzie."

It made sense. I wouldn't want people watching me puke my guts up either.

"I will," I said, finally. "I'm taking her to her next appointment. Actually, I think I'm on the hook for all of them. I know Peter won't think to offer." I paused. "My father was home when I got to the house. I can't remember a time he was home after 7:00 a.m."

"Maybe this will bring them closer. Your mom is a tough bird. She'll survive this."

"That would be just like her. Goodness knows she's not done torturing me yet." I let out a relieved snort.

"Now, I want you to take me to dinner. Maddie texted. She wants to join."

I gestured to her bag. "Don't you have to get caught up on grading?"

Sarah waved the idea away. "Nah. Half of my students don't turn their stuff in on time, so why should I?"

I reached for her hand, where it rested on my shoulder, and gave it a squeeze. "Thank you."

She leaned in and hugged me, saying nothing. What was there to say: *Sorry that your Mom, who has always been a bitch, is dying and you don't know how to process your feelings?*

"Where are we meeting Maddie?"

"A new Mexican joint. And I probably should warn you to be on your best behavior."

"Why? You afraid I'll break down and cry or something?"

She swatted my shoulder, as if appalled that I thought so lowly of her. "Not that. She's bringing a date. Do you remember the last guy you met?"

I did. He was a complete and total asshole who didn't respect women and wasn't smart enough to pretend that he did, not even while having dinner with three women. I had given him a piece of my mind—and then some. "I didn't say anything that you didn't want to say," I pouted.

"You didn't have to tell him he was an asshole to his face."

"Hey now, Maddie burst into laughter when I did. He asked us how lesbians had sex, for Christ's sake, and if we shaved our pubic hair off to avoid getting hair in our teeth while eating each other out. He's allowed to do that, but I can't say, 'You're an asshole.'"

"You do shave, by the way."

"Because I'm a neat freak, not because I'm worried about you getting hair in your teeth. It's more hygienic!"

"So it's not for my benefit at all?"

I groaned. "Good twist on that. Nicely played."

She smiled, and then started into me again. "And then you proceeded to tell Maddie's date that if he didn't understand lesbian sex, he'd never satisfy a woman."

"Well, he won't!" I stood firm on this point.

Sarah smiled. I'm sure she was relieved to see my spark back. "Just go easy on this one, okay. Maddie really likes him."

"What does he do?"

Please say teacher or something along those lines. A profession I can respect. Even a mechanic.

I admired a person who could take an engine out and put it all back together; plus, it would be nice to have one I could call.

"He's a weather forecaster on a local news channel."
Sarah turned her back. Was she deliberately avoiding my
glare?

I gawked at the back of her head as if she had
cockroaches crawling all over it. "You're joking."

"No, I'm not. And you won't make one crack about it."
She flipped around and waggled a finger in my face.

"It must be nice to have a job where you don't have to
be right—ever. Talk about job security."

"Yeah, don't say anything like that, Lizzie." She pinned
me with a stern look.

I gave a Boy Scout salute and determined that I shouldn't
say anything at all, just to be safe. Weather forecaster—please!
Did he have to train for that? I sincerely doubted it. All the
dude had to do was stand in front of a blue screen and point
to the right areas. At the least, maybe he had to study
geography.

We ran into Maddie and her date in the parking lot. After
I had been introduced to Doug the weatherman, Maddie
pulled me aside. "You okay?"

"Yeah, I'm fine. Where'd you find Doug the weather
dude?"

"Don't be an ass tonight. I like this one." She shot me a
look that suggested she'd take me out back and pummel my
ass if I was rude.

"He better not ask me about lesbian sex, then."

Maddie rolled her eyes and rejoined her date. Doug was
only about five foot nine with dark hair, eyebrows that
appeared to have been trimmed, a wispy goatee, and curious
eyes. His nose was huge. Maybe that was good for his
profession. Maybe he could smell rain or snow in the air like a
bloodhound. Was I allowed to ask that question?

The hostess seated us right away. The restaurant was
almost deserted. Either the food sucked, or the place was too
new and no one had heard of it yet; my money was on the
former, but my gut was cheering for the latter. After the day

I'd had, I really wanted something to go right.

I imagined crappy Mexican food would taste how dog food looked. I'm not saying Mexican food is only fit for dogs, just that the cheap shit, like refried beans in a can, looked like dog food. The weird watery/oily substance on top of canned beans always freaked me out.

"One of my colleagues recommended this place, so I hope it's good," Doug said, disappearing behind the oversized laminated menu.

The menu wasn't a good sign—laminated. But now that I knew Doug had suggested it, I knew I would have to pretend to love it, just to stay on Maddie's good side. I wanted to avoid an ass kicking. I think she was still a bit peeved about the last guy. But that wasn't my fault! I didn't ask him about heterosexual sex. Couldn't he be a normal guy and just watch lesbian porn, instead of interrogating the first lesbian he met in real life? Fucking creep.

"You look deep in thought, Lizzie. Care to share with the group?" Maddie always enjoyed putting me on the spot.

I straightened in my chair, ready to spill until I felt Sarah's hand on my thigh, giving me that you-better-not squeeze. Could the woman read my mind?

Maddie laughed. Doug, still engrossed in the menu, didn't notice a thing. Typical male.

"How's work been lately, Maddie?" I asked instead, biting back words about how rude her last boyfriend had been, even though I was the one being blamed for that double date crashing and burning. In our little group, I was always the fall guy. Okay, so I usually wasn't entirely blameless, but why did I have to turn the other cheek when straight people asked insulting questions? Why should they receive a pass for being noble enough to have dinner with me without having a clue how to act or what to say? Why should I just ignore their stupidity? No way.

Maddie shrugged. "Same old same old." A year ago, Maddie had opened her own interior design business, and it was growing at glacial speed. She was talented—Sarah and I had hired her when we bought our house—but the economy in this part of the country was still in the shitter. There were signs of life, but that didn't mean people were rushing out to redecorate their homes. Luckily, Maddie had her parents helping her out.

"Have you seen her work?" Doug set aside his menu and smiled like a schoolboy.

I nodded.

"That's how we met." He beamed.

Maddie colored. "Doug is one of my clients—former client." She raised a finger at me.

As if that was going to stop me.

"Are you allowed to fraternize with clients?" I arched my eyebrows, ready for battle. "Jeez, ouch!" Both Sarah and Maddie had kicked me in the shin under the table, each striking a different leg. "I was only kidding. No need for both of you to kick me."

Sarah and Maddie glared at me for outing their behavior.

Doug just chuckled. "Be glad it wasn't my sister. She can pack a wallop."

"Are you two close?" asked Sarah.

"Oh yeah. She's one year younger than me, and we've been inseparable almost since she was born."

I couldn't think of anything jerky to say about that. I had only dealt with siblings who hated each other. Both Sarah and Maddie were only children, thank God. I struggled enough with my own family; I didn't need to add any more relatives who would be disappointed in me or piss me off.

"What about you?" Doug directed the question to Sarah.

"Oh, the only sibling I have is through Lizzie, and he's an asshole."

Doug sat there with his mouth open, waiting for me to reply.

"Sarah, no reason to be shy." I looked Doug straight in the eyes. "My brother is a fucking asshole. Just ask Maddie." I pulled my legs up quickly so both Sarah and Maddie kicked each other accidentally. "Ha!"

"Why do I get the feeling I'm missing something?" Doug put the menu back down on the table.

Tilting my head, I flashed an evil grin at Maddie. "You want to field this one, boss, or should I?"

Maddie let out a long, angry breath. Shaking her head, she explained, "I met Lizzie through her brother."

"Oh, you two dated," Doug probed.

"You could say that." Maddie looked to Sarah for help, but she didn't receive any. "Truth be told, I was engaged to Peter."

Comprehension flooded Doug's face. "I wish I could say I'm sorry it didn't work out, but it worked out well for me." Maddie hugged his arm and rested her head on his shoulder. Then she stuck her tongue out at me.

Damn. I thought for sure that would get to him. I needed new ammo. "So, Doug, what do you do?"

Fire shot out of Sarah's eyes, but I did my best to free my face of all judgment.

"Meteorologist. Maddie tells me you're a history nut. Do you know who founded meteorology?" He looked innocent, even though he'd just put me on the spot.

"Uh ..." I fiddled with my fork. "Can't say that I do."

"Aristotle."

Shit! How could I say something snarky about Aristotle?

"Is that so," was all I could think to say.

Sarah and Maddie were clearly tickled pink over my inability to be an ass.

When the waitress interrupted to take our food order, I was never so happy to see a server. To make matters worse, Doug and I both ordered tamale platters—like we were two peas in the same pod. It pissed me off. Would this day never end?

"Lizzie, Maddie mentioned your mother's situation. I'm so sorry to hear it. My grandmother had colon cancer. If you ever need to talk …" He left the rest unspoken.

I sat there, frozen.

"Thanks, Doug." Sarah patted my arm and then said, "Today was her mom's first chemo session."

Why was that necessary? Why did he have to be a nice guy? I needed to vent, and the best way for me to do that was to rip other people apart. Just like my mother. Fuck! Was I turning into my mother?

Maddie directed the conversation to safer waters: the three of them discussing spring training. The Broncos lost big time in the Super Bowl earlier in the year, and everyone in Colorado hoped the upcoming season wouldn't be such a dud.

I didn't care. I just appreciated that I didn't have to speak. I really didn't think I could. Dealing with my mom and then Doug … my eyelids felt heavy. Change wasn't my forte, and I was facing a lot of it, all at once. It was best for me to tune everyone out.

Minutes later, the three of them burst into laughter. It soon became obvious that the joke involved me. I flashed a fake smile.

"I knew it. You have no idea why we're laughing, do you?" Maddie put me in the hot seat yet again.

"Maddie, you don't expect Lizzie to admit that, do you?" Sarah grinned, relishing the moment.

"I'll give you a clue: turkey baster."

I blinked foolishly, utterly clueless. Were they deriding my lack of cooking skills?

The three of them broke into a loud guffaw once again.

"Maybe Doug's sister can teach you," offered Maddie.

"How to cook?" The words spilled out before I could stop them.

Maddie roared with laughter, tossing her head so hard that it whacked the high-backed seat. She rubbed it gingerly, but she didn't stop chortling.

"My sister and her partner recently conceived their first

child," explained Doug, doing his best to control his laugher.

I still wasn't connecting the dots. Partner? That was lesbian speak for girlfriend. Was his sister gay? Damn! Was there nothing I could hate about this dude? Why did Maddie have to introduce the perfect guy today, of all days?

"Maybe I should explain this to you later," said Sarah.

Maddie laughed even harder, now gasping for breath.

"Here we are," the waitress cooed, her arms laden with plates. She set the tamale platter down before me, and I did my best to ignore Maddie's ongoing giggles by starting to eat.

To say I was miffed would be a euphemism. Sarah patted my leg, so I knew she had noticed. I bristled, moving my leg away.

She leaned over and kissed my cheek. "Don't be mad," she whispered.

I responded by shoving an overloaded fork of tamale into my mouth and chewing dramatically. As soon as I swallowed, my attitude softened.

"These are good," I mumbled, forking in another mouthful.

Doug nodded. He was chewing as enthusiastically as I was.

Sarah and Maddie, taking that as an invite, plunged their forks into our respective platters.

"Back off!" Doug uttered the exact same phrase as me and pretended to defend with his fork, just as I did. It was like we were fucking identical twins—except I didn't think my nose was as large as his.

He eyed me, brow crinkled, and gave me *the look*. Simultaneously, we each dug our forks into our date's plate and scooped up a large bite.

"Hey!" The girls protested in unison.

Doug and I high-fived. Okay, maybe I could get along with this one.

Later that night, Sarah slipped under the sheets, naked, and joined me in bed. She rested her head on my chest.

"Do you mind telling me about the turkey baster?"

She giggled and hid her face with the sheet. "Do I have to?"

"Yes." I tickled her side.

"All right, but don't flip out. Maddie was joking that you'd get me pregnant with one."

"How is that——? Oh." I didn't like the image in my head. "Um, is that how you want to ... to do it?" I didn't. Not one bit.

"Don't worry. We can't do it that way, since we're using your egg. The doctor will have to implant the embryo."

I'm sure my relief was evident.

"Gosh, you're such a weirdo when it comes to this." She poked me in the ribs.

"Comes to what?" Getting pregnant wasn't an everyday thing, at least not for lesbians.

"Gay stuff."

"What do you mean? I am gay."

"That doesn't mean you're comfortable with the topic. Not one bit." Sarah waggled a finger in my face.

"Really." I wasn't in the mood for this conversation again. My family hated that I was a lesbian, and my wife and best friend complained I wasn't gay enough; it was a losing battle.

"What about this subject instead?" I lifted her chin to kiss her. "And this one?" I rolled her on her back and licked one of her nipples.

"You happen to be quite good with this particular lesbian subject." She grinned.

"Good. Now be quiet, so I can focus."

CHAPTER FIVE

Sunday morning arrived, and I had to pinch myself to prove that the week was nearly over. Taking my mom to two appointments had really done a number on me. I knew the appointments were harder on her, and I was trying to stay focused on that, rather than on me, but as everyone loved to point out, I was self-involved. My therapist and I were working on that.

On Friday afternoon, I had received a text from The Scotch-lady. I didn't even know my mom could text!

"Pick up some more books for me. Audiobooks."

So, I had to drive to Denver once again. I wasn't one for driving—I preferred to ride my bike most places—so three round-trips from Fort Collins to Denver seemed overwhelming. I'd also hoped for a two-day reprieve from Mom. All I wanted was some time to myself, or with Sarah. That was all. Nothing more.

I rolled onto my side. The clock read seven o'clock. Seven!

Sarah nestled up against me. "You're still here."

"Yeah, I must have been more tired than I thought." I rubbed my eyes, trying to force my eyelids to stay open; they weren't cooperating.

"I kinda like it. I can't remember the last time we woke

up together. I thought when you finished grad school and started working from home, I'd see you more." Her voice was still thick with sleep.

"Don't you get tired of seeing me all the time?" I knew as soon as I finished speaking that Sarah would take this the wrong way.

She bolted upright. "Why? Are you tired of me?"

I swear Sarah could twist anything to make me look bad—not that she had to twist that statement all that much.

"That's not what I meant at all. You're a good person. It's me. For the past five minutes I've been feeling sorry for myself because my mom is sick and she's relying on me. I'm the selfish shit, not you."

That appeased her a little, but I knew I'd be walking on eggshells the rest of the weekend anyway. Just what I needed. When would I learn to keep my foot out of my mouth? Probably never.

"Can I take you to breakfast? Will that help repair the damage?"

"Do you only want to take me to breakfast to shut me up?" Sarah crossed her arms over her naked breasts. God, I loved that she always slept naked, not just in summer.

"That depends. Will it work?"

She grabbed her pillow and whacked me with it.

"Is that a yes or a no?" I tossed her pillow aside and pulled her on top of me. "Since I skipped my bike ride, how about some exercise?"

She opened her mouth to say something snarky, but I quieted her with my lips. It usually didn't take much to get her to see my line of thinking.

But today, I didn't get very far. My phone vibrated. With everything going on, I stopped to check the message, to make sure—to be blunt—that my mom hadn't died. Since I had learned about Mom, whenever I got a phone call or a text, that was my first thought.

The message was from Maddie.

"You back from your ride yet?"

Sarah sensed my drastic mood change. "Is everything okay?"

I let out a sigh of relief. "Yeah, it's just Maddie. Would you mind texting her back for me? I need to pee."

Standing in front of the sink, dousing my face with frigid water, I listened to Sarah on the phone. Texting wasn't her thing. She preferred the old-fashioned phone call. I mostly opted to text or email: the less human connection the better. How odd that my mom felt the same way.

Nope, Lizzie, block this line of thinking from your brain!

Sarah's soft footsteps sounded behind me. "Can you be ready in thirty minutes?"

"For what?" I grabbed a hand towel and dried my face.

"Breakfast with Maddie and Doug."

"She's already fucking Doug? Maddie doesn't waste any time."

"Oh, please. You slept with me right away. And, nice language," she smirked.

I sneered back at her. "That's not the point."

"What's the point, then? It's been a long time since Maddie was in a relationship. You should be happy for her." Sarah stepped into the shower and pulled me in after her.

Normally, I liked showering with her, but not when she was arguing with me. "I just don't want her getting hurt, like last time."

"Not everyone is like Peter."

"Point taken. I'll try to be happy for her, but …"

"But, what?" She lathered shampoo into her hair. This was the most dangerous part of showering with Sarah. She took the lathering process seriously and really got into it, flinging shampoo everywhere. If I didn't close my eyes, I risked being blinded by TRESemmé, or whatever brand she used.

Clenching my eyes shut, I rubbed shampoo into my own hair with much less gusto. "Doug seems nice, and you know what they say about *nice* guys." Some shampoo flew into my mouth, and I spat it out instantly.

"You think Maddie will dump him because he isn't like Peter." Sarah stood under the water to rinse, and I felt somewhat safer. Her conditioning routine wasn't so zealous. "Turn around, I'll wash your back."

I complied. "That, and ... have you seen the guy? He's not that good-looking."

Sarah smacked my ass. "Maddie isn't an asshole, like someone I know."

"Shouldn't you take that as a compliment?" I glanced over my shoulder to see her reaction.

Sarah quickly wiped a satisfied grin off her face.

"He has hairy knuckles," I continued.

"He's half Greek. He can't help that."

"Does he have a hairy back?" I pondered aloud.

"How would I know? Seriously, Lizzie! You're just trying to find things wrong with him. You can act this way all you want, but I know you like him." She raked my back with her nails. It felt good, even if she was trying to punish me.

"And he's a weatherman—they're never right about anything. He makes a living lying to people." I ignored her previous statement.

Sarah shook her head in disgust and shut the water off. "We need to hurry."

When we arrived at the Creole restaurant, located in a yellow house, I spied Maddie and Doug waiting outside with several other small groups of people. This place was always hopping.

"Morning," I said as I approached the two lovebirds. It was obvious they were in the honeymoon stage. Neither of them noticed us walking toward them; they were too busy touching each other, giggling, and sharing tender kisses.

When they did finally notice us, Maddie turned red. Doug put his hand out for a handshake.

"Maddie," a woman stuck her head out the door and

called.

"Perfect timing. Our table is ready."

I took Sarah's hand, surprising her somewhat. I wasn't going to let the lovebirds outshine me. I was already on thin ice from earlier. If I didn't act fast, I'd have to listen to Sarah complain that I didn't show enough affection in public, like Doug did.

Doug. I was competing with a man called Doug. What a preposterous name. D-ou-G.

We settled around a table more suitable for two. No complaints from me, though. I was famished. Every time we came here, Sarah ordered blackened salmon with grits and a biscuit. I usually stuck with the French toast, but today I felt adventurous. I picked up my menu, studying all the options.

"What are you doing?" asked Maddie. She rammed her menu into mine to get my attention.

"What do you think I'm doing? I'm reading the menu." I already knew what she was going to say.

"Like you'd ever order something different." Sarah scoffed, looking to Maddie instead of at me.

"Just so you know, I decided, even before we arrived, to try something new, to think outside of the box."

"What brought this on?" Maddie sipped her water, her face registering disbelief. "The craziest thing I've seen you eat are parsnips."

"Don't know. Just feel like it, I guess."

Maddie and Sarah shared a concerned look. Ever since Mom had re-entered my life, they had been sharing this look quite a bit. It was starting to irk me.

"I haven't been here before. Do you ladies have any suggestions?" The man with the ridiculous sounding name tried to come to my rescue.

While the three of them dissected the menu, I regretted my decision to tell them about trying something new. Eggs Pontchartrain. Eggs Sardou. Creole Omelet. Eggplant—what the? What happened to normal breakfast food, like French toast? Oh, wait, there was a waffle. But I knew I'd never hear the end of that one. My eyes continued the trek down the menu. The last item before the sides was sausage gravy on a biscuit with grits or potatoes. Damn. I knew I had to order the grits, even though the potatoes sounded better. Next time, Lizzie, keep your trap shut.

Sarah ordered her usual, which, as usual, put my choice to shame. Doug ordered the creamed spinach, Gulf shrimp, poached eggs and hollandaise—yuck! Maddie went for the fried eggplant with creole sauce. When I ordered, I noticed Maddie and Sarah glance down at the menu to interpret the dish's fancy name.

"Sausage gravy? You're living on the edge today," Maddie snarked.

"Hey now, at least it wasn't the French toast. Give her some credit."

I grinned my appreciation of Sarah's defense.

"Are you two ready for the big storm?" Maddie changed the subject.

I looked out the window—nothing but blue sky. Then I glanced down at my outfit—jeans, T-shirt and a fleece vest. "What storm? It's a beautiful spring day."

"Deceptive, huh." Doug sat straighter in his chair. "But in a few hours, the flakes will be flying."

"Flakes? You mean snow. It's April. How much can we get?"

"We're predicting it'll be as bad as the storm on April 23, 1885." He merrily tapped the table with his fork.

What fucking storm was he talking about? Okay, I was impressed he knew an actual date, but for all I knew he had plucked that date out of his ass. I made a mental note to look it up.

"It's going to be a blizzard." Maddie smiled at Doug, in awe of his "forecasting" abilities.

"Get out." My tone betrayed me. I immediately felt the weight of Sarah's disappointment. I had to learn to control my tone.

Maddie glared at me as if I had just smacked Doug in the face. "Care to make a friendly wager, Lizzie," she managed, through gritted teeth.

"Yeah, I do," I taunted her, waving a fork at the sky.

Next to me, Sarah bristled. Time to bring my contempt down several notches or I'd get the silent treatment for the rest of the weekend.

"One dollar."

"Oh, you are living on the edge, Maddie."

"It's not the amount, but the satisfaction. I might frame it to remind you." She looked tickled with the idea.

To Doug's credit he didn't look put out by my obvious disdain for his profession.

Profession! Puh-lease!

In my estimation, the man licked his finger, stuck it in the air, and guessed what direction the wind was blowing and what that portended. Meteorologist, my ass. I studied his massive nose to see if it twitched.

Sarah steered the conversation away from Doug by throwing me under the bus. "Lizzie doesn't think she has any issues with being a lesbian."

My heart stopped beating. "Thanks for that, Sarah," I said. I tried to stop my jaw from clenching.

Maddie laughed and covered her mouth.

"Anytime." Sarah smiled sweetly at me. This was my payback for being an ass to Doug.

Again, Doug looked comfortable. Was he slow on the uptake? Was that how he stayed calm about everything?

"I take it you had to explain the turkey baster." Maddie wasn't slow about anything.

"Yep. And then I said I wouldn't put her through that, and you should have seen how relieved she looked." Sarah rubbed the top of my head as if I were a well-behaved puppy in training.

Our food arrived, and thank God mine looked edible.

Raising my fork to dig in, I responded, "Just what issues do you think I have with being gay?"

"For starters, you just whispered the word *gay*." Maddie was quick to the punch.

"I did not!"

"Yes, you did." Sarah was feeling punchy as well.

I rolled my eyes. "Fine. What else?"

"You don't have any gay friends." Maddie sampled her eggplant. It must have passed the test because she shoveled a much larger piece into her mouth.

"That's not true. You're—"

"Bisexual. Come on, say the word with me." I assumed Maddie knew why I had stopped, but she wasn't going to let me off the hook. "Bi-Sex-U-Al."

"Now, hold on." I held my fork in midair, the tines pointing toward Maddie. "When you told me, you told me in confidence. I have no issue with saying the word."

"If I remember correctly, I said don't tell your family." She grinned triumphantly. "And you still haven't said it."

"Bisexual."

Maddie cupped her ear. "I'm sorry, what? I can't hear you."

I wanted to hurl my glass of water in her face, but two could play at this game. "Bisexual!" I roared, stabbing my diminutive pitchfork in her direction.

Every head in the place turned and stared. Not a sound could be heard.

Uh-oh. I felt the color rush to my face, and for a second thought I might pass out.

Maddie raised her orange juice in my honor. "Good for you. How'd it feel?"

I ignored her question. "So, I take it Doug knows."

Doug responded, "My sister is with a bisexual, too." He whispered the word, but I was pretty certain he did it for my benefit, since he added a wink.

Damn! I wanted to hate Doug, but I couldn't.

"Okay, so everyone else is gayer than me. I'm guessing this is something the two of you"—I stabbed my knife in Sarah's direction and back at Maddie—"have discussed and you have been waiting for the right opportunity to bring it up."

"Maybe." Sarah glanced at me out of the corner of her eye, sheepishly.

"So what? Do I need gay education or something? Do I need to tell everybody I meet that 'I'm here and I'm queer,' or should I blurt out, 'Hi, I'm Lizzie. You can remember that because it rhymes with lezzie, and I am one. Lizzie the Lezzie, pleased to meet you.'"

Sarah knew my breaking point, and she must have sensed I was approaching it. "Honey, it's not that. It's just—" She turned to Maddie for help.

"I think what Sarah is trying to say is that she's worried that when you two have a kid, well you'll raise a *you*."

"What in the hell does that mean?" I threw my fork down on my plate. Somehow, it missed the massive pile of food and clattered off the hard surface, onto the floor. Its clanging invited another round of head-turning and tut-tutting from other patrons.

"Lizzie, you know I love you, but I don't want our child to think there's anything wrong with being gay."

"And you think I'll teach our child that?"

"Not intentionally."

"But I'm too much like my family—that's what this is about, right?"

Not one of them looked at me. Doug suddenly seemed to find napkin origami captivating. Was he making a swan?

"Okay," I said.

"Okay, what?" Sarah didn't look sure what I meant.

"Okay. I see your point. What can I do … to improve?" I wasn't just trying to appease her just so I could eat my meal. Spending "quality" time with Mom made me see signs that troubled even me. I didn't want to be like her, not one bit.

"Uh ..." Sarah tilted her head to Maddie and bit her lip. Did she fear I was about to lose it completely and go bonkers? Was this the calm before the storm?

Maddie was speechless.

"So, Doug, when is your sister's baby due?" I asked, as I dipped my fork into Sarah's salmon and tried it. I couldn't stop my lips from puckering; it was horrendous. I grabbed Maddie's orange juice to wash the hideous taste from my mouth. Everyone at the table let out a relieved laugh.

I raised the OJ glass. "Welcome to our crazy meals, Doug. Just you wait, these two will gang up on you soon." I hoped so anyway. I could use some interference.

Everyone finally relaxed enough that I was able to enjoy the rest of my breakfast ... that was, until Doug nudged my arm. "Don't look now, but black clouds are rolling in."

I jerked around in my chair and squinted at the sky. Sure enough, the sky was threatening a doozy of a storm.

"Do you want to pay up now?" Maddie asked, her tone sweeter than any of the cakes that tempted from behind the glassed desserts counter.

Nothing was going my way lately.

"How about I pick up the check? Will that suffice?"

She nodded triumphantly.

CHAPTER SIX

My mother and I sat in the oncology waiting room. She was six weeks into her treatments, and her doctor wanted to have a chat. I didn't think an oncologist should call up a patient and say, "Let's have a chat." It was too broad, too worrisome.

My mom sat so still in the chair that she resembled an ice sculpture. I couldn't even hear her breathing. She stared straight ahead, prim and proper in her navy suit.

Another patient was slumped in a wheelchair off to the side, with a woman I suspected was her nurse. The patient was emaciated, wearing a scarf over her bald head and clothes that hung off a body that didn't contain an ounce of fat. I wondered if that was why Mom stared straight ahead out the window, to avoid seeing the woman in the wheelchair.

"Oh, no!"

I glanced over my shoulder to see what the commotion was about. The nurse jumped out of her chair and strode, briskly but professionally, to the front desk. She leaned over the counter and said something to the lady.

The woman behind the desk bounded out of her seat, too, and disappeared behind a door. She returned promptly, carrying pads of some sort.

That was when I figured out what happened. The poor woman in the wheelchair had peed herself. I inhaled sharply.

Incontinence. I hadn't considered that.

My mother rested her chin on her chest and briefly rubbed her eyes; then she resumed her statue pose. I thought I detected a tiny tear in the corner of her eye.

A nurse came to help wheel the woman out back, to get her out of her soiled clothes. No one spoke. Everyone did their best to pretend that everything was on the up-and-up. Not wanting to, but unable to control the urge, I glanced at the woman. She seemed clueless about what was going on. My heart startled and quivered in my chest. I feared if I opened my mouth, it would lunge out. Jesus! I wasn't prepared for this.

"Mrs. Petrie," another nurse called.

"You want me to come with?" I asked.

Mom shook her head and tried her best to march confidently into the inner bowels of the complex.

I texted Sarah, hoping she had a free period. No reply. She must have been in the middle of class. Maddie was my next choice. She texted right back, knowing I was with my mom. We exchanged a few texts: her, sympathetic, and me, relieved to stay busy and keep my mind off my surroundings. My mom didn't need me to break down right now.

Two more patients, a man and a woman, checked in, and took their seat across from me. They didn't sit next to each other, but that didn't stop them from striking up a conversation.

"How's it going?" asked the man.

"Not too bad, considering. And you? What'd the doc say last time?"

It was obvious they had run into each other before. I wondered when I would begin to recognize other patients.

"Well, I finally know. I'm terminal." The man stated it bluntly. He looked almost relieved.

I couldn't believe I was sitting in a room eavesdropping on this conversation. Weeks ago, everything in my life was going well. I was happily married to a wonderful woman who wanted to start a family. Sure, my friends drove me crazy, but I still loved them. I had published my first book, which had been well received by other historians, even if it wasn't selling. Several universities had invited me to speak about my research, and my publisher was keen for me to complete my next project. A couple of universities were even trying to convince me to join their staff. Things were good.

But now, I was sitting in an oncology waiting room and had just witnessed a man tell a stranger he was dying.

What did it feel like, to know your time was severely limited? Was he in pain? Scared?

Was my mom hearing the same news during her "chat" with the doctor?

My instinct was to run. To call Dad's assistant, have her arrange a car for my mom, and then to drive back to Fort Collins and pretend none of this was happening. To go back to my normal life—a life that didn't involve a woman pissing herself, a man confirming his imminent death, and my mother ...

I rocked in my seat, working up the courage to rise and bolt. Both hands firmly on the armrests of the chair, I began hauling my body up. I couldn't deal. And why was I expected to? Mom had treated me like shit most of my life, but now that she needed me, I was expected to take care of her.

Fucking bullshit.

Where was my father?

My brother?

She didn't need me; she needed someone to fill a role for her, to keep up appearances.

I stood. The man and woman nodded in my direction, and both smiled convincingly.

Fuck! Why couldn't I be strong, like them?

I walked out of the office and headed down the hallway. At the end was a pop machine.

I wondered if Mom might want a Sprite to help settle her stomach. I could use a drink. I put in a dollar and punched the button. The can crashed down onto the metal, the sound bringing me back to my senses. I slid in another dollar and hit the button for a Coke. After retrieving both cans, I walked back into the doctor's office. I had to be strong.

My mother stood in the middle of the room, looking for me. I held up both cans, to explain my absence. She actually looked relieved that I was still there. She grabbed my arm and I led her to the parking lot.

"I wasn't sure if you wanted a drink," I said, helping her into the passenger side of the car.

"Thank you." She took the Sprite and popped the top.

Her thank you startled me. After settling into the driver's seat I asked, "Would you like to stop anywhere on the way home?"

Mom shook her head. She stared out the window, avoiding my eyes. I wanted to ask what the doctor said, but I didn't think Mom was ready to share.

I expected her to dismiss me in the driveway, as she had all the other times, but when I pulled up to the garage, she turned to me. "Would you come in and keep me company?"

I nodded, too shocked to speak.

When I walked into my front room later that afternoon, Maddie was sitting on the couch, watching some female talk show. She clicked the TV off and bounded over to me, wrapping me up in her arms. "I thought you could use a hug." When she pulled away, she added, "Come on, I'm dying for Mexican food again. And I bet you could use a margarita or two. Sarah's meeting us there after volleyball practice."

I wanted to say thank you, but I didn't have much of a voice. Not that Maddie expected me to say anything; friends didn't.

CHAPTER SEVEN

By Friday night, I was beat. When Sarah barreled home late, after a night out with teachers from her school, I was in bed reading a book about a colon cancer survivor. That was my go-to whenever a new issue arose: I researched the hell out of it.

Sarah tilted her head to read the book title. "Any good?"

"Not sure yet." I laid the book on my chest. "How was your night? Anyone end up with a lampshade on their head?"

I went out with the teachers one night, and only one night. High school teachers had a special bond, and for some reason, they loved the job—mostly. I taught at a university while I was finishing my PhD. I preferred prep work to lecturing, which was why I decided to write stuffy books few would read. The speaking gigs helped me pay the bills. Then there was my trust fund.

"Well, Shirley got a tad bit tipsy, but nothing outrageous happened." Sarah unzipped her skirt and I watched as it slithered to the ground. "How's your mood?"

"Why?"

"I need to tell you something, and I'm not sure you'll be all that thrilled," she confessed, looking guilty.

"Huh. Is that why I'm getting a mini striptease right now?" I raised my eyebrows.

"Maybe." She began to unbutton her shirt, slowly, like a stripper, and then stopped teasing.

"Don't stop. I'm sure it'll help your cause."

"You're horrible."

"Me? You're using sex to get me to do something."

"And you're complaining. Why?"

I sat up in bed to get a better view. "Good point." I pretended to seal my lips shut and throw away the key.

"That's a good girl." Sarah eased onto my lap, and I popped open the last few buttons on her blouse.

A full moon shined brightly through the windows, so I switched my reading lamp off. The moonlight danced over Sarah's milky skin. I traced the flickering light from her chest to her stomach with one finger.

Goosebumps appeared on her body.

"Are you cold?"

She shook her head, a sexy smile on her lips. "Not one bit."

I leaned in to kiss her. Her lips felt moist, soft; the taste of beer clung to her tongue. "Who drove you home?" I asked, when we stopped for a breath.

Sarah shook her head. "Don't worry, I didn't drive. Now, shush." She smothered my mouth with hers, her passion undeniable. Overcome with excitement, I rolled her onto her back and climbed on top of her.

"Easy there. We have all night."

"I missed you," I whispered. "I feel like I haven't seen you all week, with all the traveling back and forth." I cupped her breast, watching her nipple redden and start to harden. I licked it gently, and it stood to attention in my mouth.

Trailing my right hand down the side of Sarah's body, I stopped at her ass, pulling her hips against mine. Body heat radiated from us, as Sarah slid her arms up to rip off my tank top. I stared into her eyes, unable to contemplate ever losing her.

Maybe she sensed my thought. One hand on my cheek,

she whispered, "I love you, Lizzie. I'm not going anywhere."

The words I was desperate to hear. How badly I needed to believe that. We kissed, tenderly but forcefully, as though it might be the last time we ever made love. Everything of late reminded me that it was better to live in the now; who knew what lurked around the corner?

My tongue explored her body, stopping only briefly in one spot as I descended. The insistent movement of her pelvis told me she wanted me there, but I ignored her plea. My tongue and hands explored her long, slim legs, not stopping until I reached her toes, so tiny and perfectly round.

She loved it when I kissed her toes and the soles of her feet. A spot on her lower back also drove her crazy; that was my next stop.

Rolling her over, I massaged her firm buttocks, occasionally placing a kiss here and there, my lips moving up to that special spot, which I kissed and bit tenderly.

Sarah let out a low, satisfied grumble. A pillow over her head muffled the sound. I traced the muscles of her shoulders and neck, and then kneaded them, surprised by how tense they were. My tongue flicked her earlobe and carried on its exploration.

She groaned. She wanted me now. Her hips gyrated and I heard her whisper, "please" from under the pillow.

It made me chuckle. "Okay, okay, roll over again."

Her eyes were huge, dark, and pleading as I lay beside her. She wanted me to make love to her. I ran my hand down over her breasts and stomach and then slipped a finger inside her, slowly, loving how warm she was, how moist. As I pushed deeper, Sarah arched her back and closed her eyes. I added another finger and moved in and out of her with more force, matching the rhythm of her rocking hips, pushing against her movement.

Her reaction to my being inside her always excited me. I moaned and plunged in deeper still. Sarah groaned, and before I knew it, she was inside me, too. Both of us frantically fingering in and out, deeper and deeper. Sarah was slippery with sex, each movement of my fingers against her slickening my hand. I felt the warmth of my own excitement, wet on her curled, constantly fucking fingers.

"Oh, Jesus!" I shouted. She was already taking me there with her touch. I couldn't hold on.

Her body trembled as much as mine, and her moan in my ear was satisfied. Then she collapsed on her back, exhausted, thighs quivering. I fell back too, one arm over her, my fingers still damp. Sex scented the room. I inhaled the intoxicating fragrance of it, deeply.

"Are you asleep?" I prayed she wasn't.

"No," she whispered contentedly.

"Good." I moved down the bed. My hands spread her thighs again, stroking their still-quivering paleness, and then my tongue lapped her clit.

Sarah groaned as I thrust my tongue inside her. She arched her back, circled her hips. It wouldn't take her long to come again, but I wanted to taste her. She reached down until her nails scored my shoulders, but I ignored the pain and continued lapping at her clit. I could never tire of her taste; it made my own clit throb with desire.

Sarah's grip on my shoulders intensified. She pulled me up, drawing my head back to hers, to kiss me. I slid up her body, skin on skin, clit on clit. I rubbed my clitoris against hers, both of us moaning through our kisses. I felt the tension that comes before release, Sarah's body winding itself tight before her orgasm gushed through her body. She dug her head deep into the mattress, pulling the pillow over her face to muffle her scream.

Her scream set me off, and I felt myself coming once again, too. Lights cavorted behind my eyes, and I nestled my face into Sarah's neck, letting out a long, contented sigh.

Spent, I rolled onto my side to reach for my Nalgene bottle filled with ice water. Sarah snatched it playfully, and took a long draw. Handing it to me, she said, "I love it when we fuck like that." With a sigh she collapsed back onto the bed, her hair mussed around that beautiful face.

I nodded in agreement and drank heavily from the water bottle. Settled on the bed next to her, I pulled her close. She rested her tousled head on my breast and stroked her fingers up and down my skin.

"Can I tell you the news now?" she teased.

I laughed. "Sure, I'm your prisoner now."

Resting her chin on my chest, she gazed into my eyes. "I promised Ethan we'd meet him and his family at Chuck E. Cheese's tomorrow, for Casey's fourth birthday."

"That was what you were afraid to tell me." I teased a tangle out of her chestnut hair.

"Yes."

"Dude, I'm so going to kick your ass at Skee-Ball."

"Oh, you're on, missy."

"Can you pretend that you still need to butter me up?" I winked.

"And why is that?" Hooded eyes told me she understood perfectly.

"Because I'm not done with you."

"Good!"

* * *

Walking into Chuck E. Cheese's was quite an experience. The door opened onto a cacophony of screams. Three children sprinted by us, chasing each other; a fourth rammed into my leg, bounced off, and then shouted, "Wait for me!" without apology. I wasn't sure if the boy even knew he had collided with a person.

Sarah gestured to me and laughed. "Oh, the look on your face is priceless."

I forced a smile. "I need a drink."

"Lizzie! It's ten in the morning, and this is a family establishment!"

I found her indignation endearing. "Jeez, I was just

kidding." I removed my sunglasses and squinted to block out the bright colors. It was sensory overload, especially after spending most of the night languidly making love to Sarah—not that I was complaining about that. Sarah, in a floral skirt and tight tee, looked ravishing. Was that an okay thought to have while at Chuck E. Cheese's, or did it make me a pervert, lusting after my wife? I slipped my arm around her waist and led her in search of the birthday party. Thank God I wasn't hungover, or all the shrieking would have been even more unpleasant.

"Look what the cat dragged in." Ethan stood to hug us.

"Ten o'clock. Really?" I responded.

"Naptime is at 1:30, so we didn't have a choice." He shrugged. "Besides, you're up at five every morning riding that damn bike of yours."

"Not this morning." Sarah gave me a suggestive wink.

"I've always wondered, Sarah. Does frigid Lizzie need any aids to get you going?"

I felt fire radiating up my neck to my forehead. Why did all my friends have to banter with Sarah about sex? Considering Ethan's aversion to bodily fluids, him joking about it was even harder to fathom.

"Ah, how cute. Are you Strawberry Shortcake today?" Ethan patted my back and handed me a red plastic cup filled with Coke. "Maybe this will help. The pizza will be ready in an hour or so."

Casey ran up and grabbed Ethan's hand. "Daddy, I need more tokens."

"Casey, honey. Say hi to your guests," Ethan reminded her.

I squatted on my haunches. "Happy birthday!" I put my hand out to shake.

Casey launched into my arms for a hug. Then she grabbed my hand. "Come on! Let's play!"

I looked over my shoulder. Ethan, Lisa, and Sarah all waved good-bye, smirking.

Why did this kid like me so much? She was like a cat, choosing to rub against the one person in the room who was allergic to cats. The adults sat down at the table to chat while I slipped further and further into kid hell.

"Hey, wait!"

For a moment, I was relieved. Ethan was going to save me. I stopped and turned, only to see him hurrying over with tokens. He shoved them into my hand and then turned and shouted over his shoulder, "Have fun!"

Bastard!

No wonder parents invited childless adults to parties—so we could babysit. It wouldn't surprise me if Ethan was pouring rum from a hipflask into his Coke.

"Do you like Skee-Ball?" Casey tugged on my arm to get my attention.

Skee-Ball. At least that perked me up a little. The kid was in for it now. I briefly wondered why she was dressed as a cowboy and not a princess.

"Let's go!" I squealed with delight. I stopped myself from adding, "I'll clean your clock." That didn't seem like the right thing to say to a four-year-old, on her birthday.

Five games later, Sarah showed up. She glanced down at the pathetic amount of tickets I had won. Then she eyed Casey's stash.

"I thought this was your game, Lizzie," she teased.

I growled, "I'm out of practice."

Sarah crossed her arms over her chest. "And how often did your mom and dad take you to play?"

"Obviously not enough. Besides, my nanny took me. Feel free to take over." I tossed a ball at her.

Casey ignored us. She was in the Skee-Ball zone, giggling and clapping her hands each time the machine spat out more tickets. How was I getting creamed by a four-year-old? Half the time, the ball didn't even make it to the top when Casey chucked it. She was barely tall enough or strong enough for this game, even though she was much bigger than the other kids her age. I envisioned Ethan spending a lot of time at basketball games in the near future.

Sarah pretended she was pitching a softball, and wound her arm up three times before she released the ball. It launched out of her hand and landed in the hundred-point hole. Flinging her arms in the air as if she had just crossed the Boston Marathon finish line in first place, she yelled, "Yeah."

Casey stopped briefly and squealed. Sarah put her hand out for another ball.

"Lucky shot. Let's see if you can do that again." I felt confident she'd fail.

She didn't. A machine opened up next to me, so Sarah started her own game. Within five minutes, she'd won more tickets than Casey and I combined. She ripped off her tickets and placed them in Casey's tiny hand. "Go get yourself a good prize."

Casey grabbed her tickets and then mine. I bristled, but Sarah gave me that look: the glare that said *Don't be an asshole.* It was an effective reminder.

"Come on!" Casey ran toward the prize counter.

"Don't lose her, Lizzie." Sarah pushed me in the child's direction.

I rolled my eyes. When I had a kid, I planned on getting even with Ethan. He was sitting at the table, probably having a relaxing morning, while I was chasing his child around this parent trap.

Casey had her nose and both hands pressed against the glass display case. A million tiny fingerprints speckled the glass, coupled with who knows how much slobber. When she saw me, Casey pointed to a unicorn sticker. I looked to see how many tickets she would need. Two hundred! Two hundred tickets for a measly sticker. Panicking, I thumbed through the tickets. We were seventy-five short.

"Um, Casey. We don't have enough tickets." I braced for a screaming fit in which she would throw herself down on the floor, kicking.

"Okay. Let's win more!"

I started back toward the Skee-Ball.

Casey pulled on my arm again. "Not there. Whac-A-Mole!" And she was off like a shot.

Whac-A-Mole? What the fuck?

The kid wasn't lying. There was a game called Whac-A-Mole. Armed with a club, each of us did our best to whack a mole's head whenever it popped out, smashing it before it disappeared. If we were successful, the machine would spit out part of a ticket. I could see this was going to take some time. Pushing the thought aside, I focused on the game. It would have been easier if it was an adult-sized mole-whacking table, so I didn't have to lean down so much, which restricted my arm reach.

"You're just as bad at this game."

Once again, Sarah magically appeared, just to mock me.

I handed over my mallet. "Go for it. I'm thirsty."

Before she could protest, I made a beeline for salvation. Over at the party table, Lisa was chatting with some of the moms while Ethan was reading a book. What the——? I'd been entertaining his brat while he was reading a book!

"Nice to see you're getting into the spirit." I raised the plastic cup to my lips.

"I have to take advantage of these chances. They're rare, trust me." He set the book aside. "I hear my kid kicked your ass at Skee-Ball." He grinned, knowing that would get under my skin.

"Whatever. I think she cheats."

"If that makes you feel better."

"I think the agency lied to you. There's no way she's four. Has to be five."

Ethan stared at me as if I was insane. "Do you only play Skee-Ball with children under the age of five, so you can win?" He quirked an eyebrow.

"Lizzieeeeeee!"

The voice made me jump. The kid was back, ready to

whisk me off again. Ethan smirked as he picked up his book.

"Come on!" Casey shouted.

She dragged me to a pit filled with plastic balls. What was the point of this? Casey climbed right in. "Get in!"

Get in? There was no way I was climbing into that disgusting germ factory.

"Don't be a scaredy-cat!" Casey taunted me.

Scaredy-cat? She did not!

I jumped in, feeling silly. None of the other adults were in the ball pit. Oh well, they were scaredy-cats.

Casey dived under the balls and then popped back up again, just like a grinning little mole, squealing in delight. Honestly, I didn't see the appeal, but her infectious laughter wore me down. Soon, I was mimicking her. I would go under, holding my breath, and then jump out like a monster and try to grab her. Other kids came over. Before I knew it, I was entertaining half a dozen kids, all by acting like a complete idiot. I walked about like a zombie, stumbling through the brightly colored balls, mumbling, "I'm going to get you."

A child would draw near, and then dash off, screaming. Another would approach timidly, running off after I repeated the whole zombie routine. I wish I could say I was bored out of my mind, but I wasn't. Not once in all that time did I think of my mom. All I did was let go and have fun.

"Come on, Casey, time for lunch!" Sarah helped Casey out of the ball pit. "Lizzie, say good-bye to your friends." Sarah was enjoying herself way too much.

I waved to my playmates. They waved back and then began a new game. Jeez, they could have missed me a bit more. Ingrates.

"You fit in here." Sarah looped her arm through mine.

"Are you surprised?" I raised my eyebrows.

"Stunned." She patted my arm. "And thrilled."

I rolled my neck back and forth. "I think I pulled a muscle playing Whac-A-Mole."

"Oh, poor baby. I'll give you a massage later. Maybe

more."

"Maybe. But I'm beat."

"One hour playing with Casey and you're turning me down."

"I'm sure you'll be able to rally me later. You do have a certain charm about you."

She walked ahead of me, swaying her hips more than usual.

"How come she's not Ariel today?" I asked as I plunked myself down next to Ethan, gesturing to Casey's outfit.

"*Toy Story* is her new thing."

"*Toy Story*?"

"Seriously, you haven't seen that one either?" Ethan bit into his slice of pizza. A long string of cheese suspended itself from his chin. When I motioned to it, he wiped it away daintily with a paper napkin. "She's dressed as Woody. The cowboy in the movie."

Damn, now I needed to watch another juvenile cartoon.

"How long is this movie?" I asked, not sure why. Did I plan on sneaking off to the bathroom to cram it in, just so I could show up a four-year-old?

Ethan's forehead wrinkled. "How long? I don't know. But I should mention there are three of them."

"Three!"

"The third one was nominated for Best Picture."

"Yeah, right." I rolled my eyes. I wasn't falling for that one.

"I'm serious." He pulled out his phone and brought up the wiki article.

"Shit!" I clapped a hand over my mouth.

Ethan chuckled. "Don't worry. We're teaching her curse words are just words, trying to take the power out of them."

"Let me know how that works out for you," I winked.

"Have you considered joining a soon-to-be parents group?"

I studied his face to determine whether he was kidding.

He wasn't. Even the thought of it made me uncomfortable. "Should I?"

"I didn't, but you might want to."

"Uh-huh. Because everyone thinks I'm going to crash and burn," I said bitterly.

"Not true. We want you to succeed. Trust me, we're all pulling for you." He stared across the table at our wives, hesitated, and then asked, "How's your mom?"

CHAPTER EIGHT

My cell rang at four in the morning. Fumbling to grab it, I accidently knocked it onto the carpet. Sarah flicked on her bedside lamp.

"Who is it?" Her voice was raspy with sleep.

I shrugged, too busy locating the ringing phone. "Hello," I finally said.

"Lizzie?"

"Yes." I sat up in bed.

My father never called me, so I knew the news was bad.

"It's your father. I'm at the hospital with your mom."

I wanted to ask how bad it was, but I couldn't force myself to utter the question.

"Lizzie ... you there?"

"Yes. I'm sorry the phone cut out," I lied. "I'll be there as soon as I can."

"Thank you," he said, and then I heard a click.

Thank you. My father wasn't the type to say thank you. This was bad.

Sarah wrapped her arms around me. She had nuzzled up next to me to hear the conversation. Normally, that type of behavior would annoy the shit out of me, but now I didn't mind. It saved me from having to vocalize what was going on.

Was this it?

I rubbed my eyes forcefully and then chastised myself for lollygagging. This wasn't the time for contemplation; it was the time for action.

I jumped out of bed and grabbed up my jeans from where they lay crumpled next to the bed, not even bothering to locate underwear. Sarah followed suit, tugging on a wrinkled skirt. At first, I was going to tell her not to bother, that I'd go alone, but then I realized I wanted her there. My eyes felt briny, tearing over no matter how hard I tried to stop tears from forming.

Before pulling our car out of the garage, Sarah said, "Hang on a second."

She threw open the car door and ran back inside, reappearing with one of my Nalgene bottles, which I usually kept in the fridge for my early morning rides. She plopped the bottle in the cup holder by the gearshift and then backed the SUV out of the garage. Immediately, I reached for the bottle, hoping water might force my sobs back down.

Neither of us had said a word after the phone call. Actually, I was pretty amazed by our efficiency. We were dressed and out the door in less than five minutes. Sarah even managed to brush her teeth. I opted for a quick rinse with mouthwash.

There was little traffic on the way to Denver; few people were up and out the door so early on a Sunday. The GPS led us right to the hospital entrance.

"Do you want me to drop you off?" Sarah asked.

The million-dollar question. Sarah hadn't seen my family since Peter's wedding. So far, Mom seemed content to ignore the big purple elephant in the room, and I wasn't trying to force the issue.

"I'm sure the cafeteria is open. I can hang out there." She was trying her hardest to make the decision easy for me.

All I had to do was nod and be done with it. A simple nod would make it clear Sarah would take no part in my family interactions, and she was giving me the okay to make that decision. I knew Sarah wasn't the type to throw a hissy fit to get her way, not at a time like this. Because the circumstances were different this time around: my mother could be dying, right at this moment. And right at this moment, I wanted Sarah there. I knew I wouldn't be able to do it without her. I had an urge to shout, *Look at me! I'm growing up*. But I still couldn't speak.

I motioned for her to find a parking spot. Then, as we were getting out of the car, I reached for her hand. Together, we headed toward the sliding glass door.

As soon as we were inside, I released her hand; maybe I wasn't growing as much as I thought.

Mom was in the cancer ward. Cancer Ward. Capital C. Capital W. It was still a shock to my system to hear that word: cancer.

I knew it was silly. I had been taking Mom for chemo treatments for weeks, and to the oncologist's office for checkups. But for the most part, I had blocked out the nasty word. I had wiped away the reality and focused on the little things.

Pick up Mom.

Take Mom to her appointment.

Wait for the appointment to end.

Take Mom home.

It was the only way I could avoid the gravity of the situation and still function. Compartmentalizing helped me stay strong. I lied to myself. I said I was doing it for my mother's sake. Mom didn't need to see her daughter breakdown. But I knew deep down that it was more for my sake than hers.

My father stood outside the room. After shaking my hand, he turned to Sarah. "Thank you for coming. It's good to know Lizzie has someone ... well, you know."

I didn't know how to handle that statement; from the look on Sarah's face, she didn't either. My father was a man of few words. He had said more to me in the past few weeks than he had during my entire childhood.

"How is she?" I finally spoke. Even to me, my voice sounded thick, like I was drunk.

"She's resting at the moment."

"What happened?" Sarah took over, speaking on my behalf.

"Evelyn discovered some swelling on her arm, near the chemo port. She's being treated for Deep Vein Thrombosis."

I nodded, not absorbing the information. Evelyn! I always forgot Mom had a name. For years, I thought of her only as The Scotch-lady, nothing more.

Evelyn.

Her name made her real to me.

My father continued. "DVT is the fancy term for blood clot. They're worried it can get into her bloodstream and work its way into her lungs, which would cause a pulmonary embolism. Right now, they're doing their best to thin her blood to liquefy the clot."

Pulmonary embolism. Why did all of these medical terms have to sound so fancy and intimidating? *Deep Vein Thrombosis.* Were they purposefully trying to scare the shit out of their patients and their family members?

"When did she notice the swelling?"

I admired Sarah's ability to hold it together and to be able to speak.

"In the middle of the night. She hadn't been sleeping well," he explained. "I would have called earlier, but she didn't want me to." He stared into my eyes, shrugged. "You know your mother." Then he added, "Peter's on his way."

On the inside, I was screaming, but I nodded crisply to my father. His stoic expression never changed. As a distraction, I tried to remember a time when my father had shown emotion, even a tiny flicker. But it was to no avail. I couldn't.

Still, I shouldn't be too hard on the man. He was finally speaking to me—not that he was verbose with Peter either.

My father usually let his wife do all the talking. Now that she was sick, he was stepping up to the plate, finally.

"Would anyone like coffee?" asked Sarah.

"Yes, please." My father turned to her, his expression still blank. "Thank you."

"I'll go with you." I looked at my father. "Shall we get Peter one, as well?"

"Two actually. His fiancée is coming with him." He didn't wait for me to respond to the announcement. Instead, he just turned and walked back into my mother's hospital room.

I stared at the door that had just shut in my face. Sarah tugged on my arm, trying to dislodge the fog that had descended on my brain.

Fiancée?

Farther down the hallway, when I thought it was safe enough, I asked Sarah, "Did Maddie mention that my brother was getting married?"

Sarah shook her head.

"Why is it that every time my brother reenters my life, he has a fiancée?"

In reality, it had only happened twice. My brother and I were not best buddies, so it wasn't overly shocking that I didn't know.

"I'm not surprised, really. Peter always wanted a perfect life." Sarah avoided my eyes, fixing her gaze on the signs at the end of the hallway. "I think there's a coffee shop this way." Once again, she had to yank on my arm to get me moving. My brain and my feet weren't on speaking terms.

We discovered a Starbucks' trolley near the entrance, and I ordered four coffees, plus a chai for myself. Sarah was smart enough to load her pockets with different types of sugar packets and creamers.

On the way back, I stopped in my tracks. "Should I get anything for Mom?"

"I doubt she can have coffee at the moment." Sarah

didn't sound convinced.

"She's been drinking a lot of herbal tea lately. I'll get one. The last thing I want to do is hurt her feelings."

Sarah gave me an odd look, but said nothing.

Before we turned the corner near my mother's room, I heard Peter's booming voice in the hallway. Jesus, didn't he understand this was a hospital? Sarah's expression said *Just don't say anything rude.*

I smiled at her reassuringly. Inside my brain, *Just be nice, Just be nice* was running on a loop. *Just be nice. This will be over with soon. Just be nice.*

Peter towered over my father, who, surprisingly, looked much smaller than when I had I seen him minutes earlier.

What was this like for my father? His wife of thirty-something years was in a hospital bed and, from what I heard from Maddie a few years ago, my father had been seeing the same mistress for years.

Peter must have heard our footsteps. He stopped talking and eyed me menacingly, a perplexing smile turning up the corners of his mouth. The last time I had seen my brother, Maddie jilted him at the altar. His eyes told me he hadn't forgiven my betrayal in leaving the wedding with Maddie.

"I wasn't sure what everyone wanted, so I hope plain coffee will do."

Sarah handed a cup to everyone, including a woman in a pink sundress.

"This is fine." My father removed the lid and blew into the steaming black liquid. It was odd, seeing my father do this. It made him human, vulnerable. My father, Charles Petrie, had to wait for his coffee to cool, just like everyone else.

"We picked up some sugar packets and creamer." Sarah emptied her pockets and placed the loot on a small table in the hall.

The woman in pink snatched up two fake sugars and dumped them in her cup, swirling them in with a wooden stir stick. Peter, who wore golf clothes—yellow pants with a purple shirt that could only look good on the Easter Bunny—passed on the sugar. I think the Easter Bunny would have been too proud to wear that outfit.

"Hi, I'm Sarah. And this is Lizzie—Peter's sister." Sarah offered her hand to the stranger dressed in pink.

The woman hesitated.

"Where are my manners?" Peter interrupted. "I'm so sorry. Elizabeth, I would like you to meet my fiancée, Tiffany."

My brother always insisted on calling me Elizabeth. I bristled at that, and at the fact that he hadn't bothered to introduce my wife, Sarah. *Just be nice.*

"Hi, Tiffany."

The woman spoke for the first time. "It's Tie-Fannie."

I tilted my head to catch the pronunciation. "*Tiff*-any?" I repeated, knowing full well that was not what she had said.

The pink lady shook her head and gave a fake smile. "No. It's pronounced more like Tie-Fannie."

Tie-Fannie. It wasn't bad enough that my brother was nearing forty and going to marry a chick who looked barely twenty-two, but he had to find a *Tiffany* who was so conceited she made up a whole new pronunciation of her name.

"Oh, how unusual. Is that a family name?" asked Sarah in a sincere tone.

Tiffany smiled, not responding. Maybe she didn't want to ruffle Peter's feathers. I was pretty certain Peter would have filled her in on his version of the jilted-at-the-altar story, leaving out that he was cheating on Maddie. He probably hadn't yet informed his new fiancée that he had no intention of being a faithful husband. No doubt that detail was superfluous to my brother.

"You never could count, Elizabeth," said Peter.

Count? How was this connected to his strange fiancée and the pronunciation of her name? I frowned.

Peter nodded to my mother's tea.

"Thanks, Peter. I completely forgot I got Mom a tea."

"Tea?" scoffed Peter. "Did you add scotch to it?"

Even Tiffany looked at Peter like he was a moron.

"That was very thoughtful, Lizzie. Your mom just asked for a tea." My father took the cup from me and disappeared into the hospital room.

Peter looked triumphant. Both of us knew I wouldn't get the credit for the tea. But I didn't give a damn.

"Dad said only two people are allowed in the room at a time. Would you mind if Tiff and I go first? I have a golf date with some clients." Peter sipped his coffee, an odd twinkle in his eye.

It took everything I had not to laugh in his face. *Just be nice, Lizzie.*

"Not a problem, Peter." I waved him in, and then turned my back on him and headed for a few chairs at the end of the hallway.

"It was wonderful meeting you, Tie-Fannie." Sarah stressed the pronunciation without a hint of mockery.

Sarah and I settled into the chairs. Soon, my father joined us after Peter and Tiffany entered the room.

"Your mother said thanks for the tea." For a second, I thought my father was going to pat my knee, but he pulled his hand away.

"When did Peter get engaged?" Sarah asked.

For a split second, I thought I saw a trace of disapproval in Dad's body language. "A couple of months ago."

"Have they known each other long?" probed Sarah.

My poor father probably wasn't used to being interrogated by anyone, especially about these types of matters. "A year," he grunted.

Sarah stopped her questioning and pulled out her cell phone. Was she texting Maddie? Hopefully not. I would like to break that news to her in person, not that she'd care all that much, not now that she had Doug the weatherman.

The three of us sat silently until Peter and Tiffany approached. "Elizabeth, the nurse said Mom needs to rest for a bit before you can see her."

Sarah and I remained in our seats. I seethed. Why did he always insist calling me Elizabeth, knowing full well I didn't like it?

My father rose and Peter shook his hand, business-like. "Dad, let us know if you need anything. I would skip this damn golf game if it wasn't so important." He puffed out his chest like a soldier. Did he really think a game of golf superseded his mother being in the hospital? How pathetic.

Peter always tried to appear more important than he was. True, he made a lot more money than me, but did that really matter? Both of us had trust funds, and neither of us had to work, really. But he stood in front of us posing as though the entire world as we knew it would collapse if he didn't rush off immediately.

My father escorted them to the elevator.

"What a jackass," I whispered to Sarah.

She covered her mouth, trying to look concerned rather than amused. "You know, Peter."

"Pompous prick." I sat up in my chair and mimicked, "I would skip the damn golf game—"

Then my father stood before me, and I felt the blood rush to my face.

Dad didn't say anything. He sat down next to me and stared straight ahead.

"How long will she be in the hospital?" Sarah tried to bury my *faux pas*.

"A few days, at least." Dad's voice was strong, but it carried a tinge of sadness. I got the impression he wanted to breakdown, except he didn't know how.

"I can stop by the next few days and keep her company," I offered. The idea of my mom alone in the hospital was an unbearable thought. I knew from my own battle with Graves' Disease how scary it was to deal with an enemy that showed no mercy. My thyroid condition was treatable, but it didn't have a cure. And it wasn't nearly as scary as cancer, certainly not in my opinion.

"Thank you. I would appreciate that. I think it'd be all right for you two to visit with her. The nurse said it was okay."

Wait? The nurse said it was okay? Had Peter lied to stall my visit? Was Peter trying to ruin whatever plans I had for the day? Not that I had any. And if I did, I would have canceled them, considering. What a conceited jerk.

Sarah stood and waited for me. I hadn't intended on asking her to actually visit with my mother, but after my father suggested the two of us should head in, I couldn't refuse. I always wondered whether my father really gave a damn that I was gay. He hadn't ever said a word either way. I added it to the list of things I didn't know about the man: whether he believed in God, whether he had a favorite football team, whether he preferred dark or milk chocolate, or, just anything, really? My father was a stranger. The only reason I knew his middle name was because I'd peeked at his passport when I was a child.

My mother. Well, that was a completely different story. I knew how Mom felt about me. Mom voiced her opinion, usually a negative one, all of the time. Whenever she had a chance, she took a dig at me for being a lesbian.

Les-Bi-An: that was how she pronounced it. Akin to an odious disease, like leprosy in biblical times.

Sarah paused right outside the door, and I let out a long breath and steadied my nerves. She gave me a mischievous smile, and all of a sudden I felt confident. I winked at her as we strolled in together to visit The Scotch-lady.

Mom lay in the hospital bed, resembling a shriveled, featherless bird. Her skin was pasty pale. No makeup hid her flaws or wrinkles. Her hair was still in a bun, but strands fell down haphazardly. The only way to describe how she looked was frail. Or, beyond frail, as in knocking on death's door.

Her eyes flicked open feebly, and she saw Sarah standing next to me. Her expression didn't contort with anger, but there was no warmth there either.

Feeling silly that I was gawking at her like she was a specimen under a microscope, I took the seat next to her bedside. "How you feeling?" I immediately cringed, knowing how she would respond. Why did I constantly ask her that question?

"How do you think?" came her curt reply.

I tried to console myself. At least she retained some of her usual anger; that might keep the fire going for a bit longer.

"Is there anything I ... we can do to make your stay easier?" I motioned to Sarah. My mother hadn't even acknowledged her. At least my wife wasn't wearing a fucking pink dress and telling everyone they should pronounce her name Sa-Rah.

Mom motioned to the table at one side of her bed. One of the novels I had purchased for her recently sat there, pages down, the spine sitting up. "My eyes are too tired. Can you read to me?"

Tears began to well in my eyes, but I willed them away. "Sure."

"You"—she shocked the hell out me by motioning to Sarah—"can I have more tea?"

It wasn't the best progress, but at least she had admitted Sarah was in the room with us. I wouldn't have put it past my mother to ignore her completely.

"Of course, Evelyn," Sarah said without a glance at me, but her body language told me she thought this was a big step as well. Not that either of us pined for my mother's acceptance, but if we could live without strife, it would be something.

I read to my mother for several minutes before Sarah returned. By the time she peeked in, holding a steaming cup of herbal tea, the patient was fast asleep. Sarah sat down on the other side of the bed, not speaking. We both kept Mom silent company for an hour.

When Dad shook my hand as I said good-bye, I swear he

held onto it for an extra second.

Was I imaging all of this? My mother had spoken to Sarah—negatively, sure, but she still spoke to her. My father hadn't exactly said, "Hey, I'm cool with the fact that you're a lesbo." But he had ushered Sarah into Mom's room and he had said he was glad I had someone.

Jesus! Why did I care?

And then there was Peter. What a fucking asshole.

By the time we got outside, I was worked up.

"A pink dress? Who wears a pink dress to the hospital?" I fumed.

Sarah stood back to avoid my flailing arms.

"It's early ... on a Sunday. It wasn't like she was out and about and then rushed on over. Nope. She got a phone call just like us, and she intentionally put on a *pink* dress. My brother's bimbo actually got out of bed and slipped into a pink sundress to visit her future mother-in-law in the cancer ward. Un-Fuck-Ing-Believable!" I ranted, walking along the curb, following it as though I was in the circus and it was my tightrope. Spying a pop can in the gutter, I attempted to kick it. My foot soared over the top, causing me to lose my balance. I stumbled off the curb and landed on my ass.

Sarah tried to muffle her laughter.

That annoyed me. Instead of getting up and admitting I was acting like an ass, I lay down and stared at the gray sky above. Clouds threatened rain. Passersby threw me odd looks, and I did my best to return a snarky stare.

"Are you done?" Sarah finally asked.

"With what?" I barked.

"Throwing a fit?" Sarah loomed over me.

"No," I pouted.

"Lizzie, your mother is in the hospital. This isn't the time to act like a child. You're mad at Peter. I understand. But get a grip, will ya!"

"Mad at Peter? What're you talking about? Tie-Fannie is the one who wore pink." I let out a derisive snort.

"Oh, come on, you couldn't give two shits about what she wore. You're mad that Peter swooped in and did his usual Peter thing: acting like he was in charge and super important. He has a wonderful way of making you look like an ass."

"Does not." I tried to stop my face from scrunching up in anger.

"Really? Then tell me the real reason you're lying in the gutter."

"Gutter!" I bolted up.

Sarah tugged my arms and helped me to my feet. "Come on. Let's go get some food in you so we can come back this afternoon for visiting hours."

* * *

That night we had dinner plans with Maddie, Doug, and Rose. I wasn't in the mood for company.

"Maybe you should go without me." I tucked my hands into my jeans and stared intently at the floor, searching for an escape route. "I won't be good company tonight."

"Oh, honey. You're never good company." Sarah lifted my chin with her hand. "I don't think you should be alone tonight. You brood all day long when I'm at work." She winked at me.

"Brood—is that what you call research?" I attempted a weak smile, but I couldn't muster the energy.

"Come on. I need your help breaking the news to Maddie."

Her face said that was her final word. I had to go, or we'd be heading for a conversation later. And not a friendly chat—one of those talks Sarah said was supposed to be helpful but was actually anything but. I already knew I had shortcomings. Did we need to have a conversation to point them out? I preferred leaving things unsaid; Sarah didn't. Ever since I almost lost her, I realized that maybe her method was better. Didn't mean I liked it, though. Not. One. Bit.

My therapist agreed with Sarah. She encouraged open

dialogue with my wife. Dialogue. It made it sound like we were diplomats trying to solve the Middle East Crisis. Not that our problems were that severe, thank God.

"Shall we order some bottles of wine?" Rose asked, after perusing the menu of the new Italian place the girls had read about in the local paper.

Their mission to try every restaurant in northern Colorado was starting to wear on me. Personally, I could eat at the same place every night of the week and be perfectly content. Once I found something I liked, I stuck with it. But those two loved change. Mixing things up scared me.

When Sarah's best friend, Haley, moved to California two years ago, Sarah and Maddie became almost inseparable. Maddie was still reeling from Peter, and Sarah had lost her best friend. Usually, their need to hang out all the time didn't bother me. But it did tonight. Why couldn't we stay at home so I could mope and eat a gallon of mint-chocolate-chip ice cream?

"Yes," responded Sarah. "I'm thinking red. Mom, you choose. You're so good at pairing wine with food."

While Rose ordered the wine, Maddie eyed me. "How's your mom, Lizzie?"

I shrugged. "She seems okay, given the circumstances. At least they don't have her hooked up to a bunch of machines—not sure I can take that. They've increased her Coumadin dosage, and they're monitoring the blood clot."

Rose and Maddie gave me sympathetic smiles, and Sarah rubbed my back. Then she turned to Maddie. The look in her eye said, *It's time to tell her.*

"We saw Peter," she said.

Maddie did her best not to react, but she did. I was pretty sure Doug noticed, although he tried to remain unperturbed. What an awkward situation. Really.

"How is the busy worker bee?" Maddie asked in a breezy tone.

"He had to rush off for a round of golf," I sneered.

Doug raised his eyebrows. I wondered how much he knew about my family. Probably enough. Maddie was chatty, just like Sarah. No wonder the two of them hit it off so well.

"You're kidding." Maddie chewed her lower lip, not in surprise but in contempt. "That's so Peter."

The waiter arrived and did the ridiculous routine of opening the bottle and letting Sarah's mom sample the wine. I hoped the process might distract Sarah, but knew, deep down, that it wouldn't.

Sarah patted my thigh. Then she dove headfirst into the danger zone. "He wasn't alone."

Rose's face scrunched up. Sarah's mom hadn't met any of my family, and I was fairly confident she never wanted to. The Petries were not high on many invite lists. They attended business functions, but friends? No. We didn't have any family in the state. It was just the four of us.

"Really?" Maddie's face looked curious. "Let me guess … much younger than me."

I laughed, but quickly tried to pretend I was coughing.

"Don't worry, Lizzie. I know your brother. Shall we play a game?" Maddie tapped her fingernails on her water glass. "She's blonde?"

Sarah nodded. Doug withered in his seat. Was he upset for Maddie, or for himself?

"Under twenty-five?"

Again, Sarah nodded.

"Ditzy?"

"She wore a pink sundress to the hospital," I stated.

"Dear me." Rose shook her head in disgust.

Maddie wrinkled her brow, thinking of the next question, but Sarah stopped her. "There's something you should know."

Doug opened his mouth, and I could see bits of half-chewed bread and wondered if he was trying to keep his mouth busy so he wouldn't speak out of turn.

Sarah turned to me, as if I should make the big

announcement because Peter was my brother. Gee, thanks. I sat up in my chair and placed both hands on the table, bracing myself for the bomb I was about to drop.

Maddie's face paled.

Rose held a wineglass to her mouth, not sipping it. All eyes were on me.

I cleared my throat. "It seems that Peter is ... engaged ... again."

No one spoke. No one moved. Doug's mouth stayed open. Rose still held her wineglass to her lips. Sarah watched Maddie.

Maddie stared out the window. I wasn't sure she was breathing, and I tried to see if I could see her taking a breath (without being obvious that I was staring at her chest). Everyone was so still I felt as if we were trapped in a photograph.

"I ... " The rest of my words stayed buried inside.

Maddie wadded up her napkin, threw it on the table, and then jumped out of her seat, knocking over her chair. With one hand over her mouth, she dashed out of the restaurant. Sarah leaped to her feet and chased after her. Rose glared at me as if I were the guilty party.

I wanted to joke, "Don't shoot the messenger," but Rose's former threat to run me over with her car popped in my head, silencing me.

Doug stared at the fork in his hand and traced some of the lines of the tablecloth with the tines.

"I think *some* families are more trouble than they're worth," stated Rose, grasping her wineglass, white knuckled, and bringing it jerkily to her lips. Her emphasis was directed at me, of course. I clenched my jaw and remained mute. I had no leg to stand on. I would be the last person to come to my family's defense.

"I'm not sure all families are that bad," responded Doug, weakly.

Rose nodded. "Sarah and I get along well."

"I'm best friends with my sister, and I'm close with my parents." Doug perked up some, straightening in his chair.

So, that left me. Only *my* family was fucked up. My brother was the reason Maddie had run from the restaurant like it was on fire.

Rose studied me closely, waiting for an opportunity to dig in her claws. I felt like a fox in a trap. Would she skin me alive?

"Uh, I think I'll go check on Maddie." I lurched out of my seat and rushed off before Rose or Doug could react.

I found them in Maddie's BMW. It wasn't cold out, but I'm assuming they wanted some privacy.

Sarah rolled down the passenger side window when I approached. I leaned down and patted Sarah's hand, where it rested on the car. "Everything okay?"

Maddie sniffled. "I don't know why I'm so upset."

Her reaction shocked me, but I sensed I should keep that thought to myself. My therapist kept telling me that my childhood prevented me from reacting to things like a normal person. She didn't say it like that, of course. She used much fancier lingo, to spare my fragile feelings. But that was the gist. My family fucked me up, and I cut myself off from others so I wouldn't get hurt.

"Don't be hard on yourself. Your reaction is normal." Sarah rubbed Maddie's back. Maddie leaned on the steering wheel. It made me think of drawings I'd seen of torture devices in the Middle Ages: a person prostrated on a rack and then gutted or quartered.

"Peter's an ass. When I walked out, I had no intention of ever seeing him again." Maddie's voice informed me she was barely in control. "So why do I care?"

I was wondering the exact same thing. Why was she facedown on the steering wheel, moaning about Peter marrying some young gold digger? Good riddance, if you asked me.

"Because you're human, Maddie." Sarah didn't look at

me, but I wondered if she guessed my thoughts.

What a shitty day. First the hospital, and then Rose hinting that out of everyone at the table only I had the effed-up family, and now Sarah was hinting that I wasn't human.

Maddie slumped back against her seat, her face streaked with tears and snot. I cringed at the sight. Sarah searched the glove box, locating some tissues and passing them to Maddie, who started to clean herself up.

After a few moments, Maddie opened the driver side door. "Might as well go back in. Poor Doug."

I followed the two women in, feeling pretty shitty. Fuck Peter! He had messed up this whole day for me. The only person who had been civil to me the entire day was my father, and that was because the man never talked much. He had the right idea. I could relate to that; could respect it, in fact.

Doug stood and helped Maddie to her seat. Why was Maddie so upset about Peter when she had a nice guy like Doug? Sure, he had a big nose, but he wasn't wearing purple and yellow together.

"Thank you." Maddie placed a reassuring hand on Doug's shoulder.

"Can I get you anything, dear?" asked Rose. "Would you like a stiff drink?"

"Thank you, Rose. I'm fine. A bit embarrassed, really. Not sure why I reacted that way." Maddie smoothed the napkin on her lap.

"Well, the news could have been delivered better." Rose gave me the stink eye.

Wait a minute. Sarah had started it. She was the one who made me deliver the *coup de grace*. Why place the onus on me? If it were up to me, I wouldn't have said anything at all. Sarah's human need to share had got me into this mess. Maybe it *was* best to be a robot, like my father.

And how else was I supposed to deliver the news? Would sugarcoating it have worked better? Should I have said, "Well, there may be a chance that the two of them may be more serious than boyfriend/girlfriend … I don't mean wedding bells, but, oh, okay, I do."

The news had to be delivered, so I delivered it—at Sarah's prodding.

"Let's talk about something else." Maddie flashed a sad smile. "Something happy."

"I made an appointment with the fertility clinic to get the process started," Sarah said, as if that was normal dinner conversation. Did she really want to talk about sucking my eggs out of me and then putting one in her after mixing in some semen to make a baby cake?

"That's great news," Doug said. He looked like he meant it, as if he wasn't even grossed out by the process.

What was wrong with these people?

"When's the big day?" asked Maddie, obviously relieved that I was now in the hot seat.

"Not until September."

"Wait. What?" I said, without thinking. The months were flying by and September was just around the corner.

Sarah leaned closer to my ear. "I told you I was going to make the appointment." Her tone suggested I shouldn't start a scene.

"I know, I just didn't think …"

"Here we go," said Rose. She motioned to the waiter for another bottle of wine.

Sarah crossed her arms and Maddie eyed me with a look that warned *tread carefully*. Only Doug had kind eyes. Sympathetic eyes. I was starting to really warm to Doug the weatherman.

"Now, don't all gang up on me. It's not what you think."

"Please, Lizzie, tell me what I'm thinking." Sarah's sarcasm shot through me. I knew I was in serious shit now, for the second time that night. And I was innocent. I pictured myself being hauled off by bailiffs. After being sentenced to death, I shouted, "I'm innocent, I tell you. Innocent!"

"Sarah, I'm on board with the whole egg thing—"

"Egg thing? That's how you refer to our child?"

Oh boy. I wanted to say, "Fasten your seatbelts, it's going to be a bumpy ride," to help ease the tension, but one look at her face told me that would be a mistake.

I tugged on my collar and took a sip of water, unsure how to get out of this mess.

"I made sure the appointment didn't coincide with one of your mom's."

I nodded, remembering her asking for my mom's hospital appointment schedule. We kept a calendar on the fridge, so we could keep track of each other's schedules and avoid situations like this. Sarah started writing everything down on the calendar and there was some type of code that I couldn't decipher but never asked about.

"What day of the week is the appointment?" I held my breath.

"Monday."

Whew!

"That's great!" I thought my enthusiasm would make her feel better. I was wrong.

"What plans do you have that you don't want to tell me about?"

"It's not that."

I heard Doug shift in his seat, and Maddie cleared her throat menacingly. I have been known, in the past, to keep secrets from Sarah. "I just spaced it, with everything going on."

The waiter arrived to take our orders. The poor man had been waiting forever, given all of our previous drama. Rose waved him away. I made a mental note to give him a big tip, since we were taking up so much of his time. By now, we should have been enjoying our main course; instead, we hadn't even started eating.

"I've been invited to speak at a conference at a small university in California. The symposium is on a Friday, so I was hoping you could fly in that night, because the university is near Napa Valley. I thought it would be good for the two of us to have a weekend away together, before you're pregnant."

Sarah's eyes softened.

"I'm sorry. I got the call last Thursday, when I was at one of my mom's appointments. I totally spaced out about putting it on our calendar. It wasn't until you mentioned the appointment that I even remembered the commitment. That would have been embarrassing—if I didn't show up." I coaxed her back around with a silly grin.

"Why didn't you just spit it out, Lizzie?" asked Rose, too busy snapping her fingers at the poor server to bother waiting for my response. She was ready to eat, and she was fed up with me.

So Sarah could just spit out news about our medical appointments, but I couldn't spill the news that Peter was getting married? I never knew how to act around Rose anymore. Sarah leaned over and whispered in my ear, "I heart you."

CHAPTER NINE

The next day, I found Tiffany sitting at Mom's bedside in the hospital. Mom was napping. I nodded hello, not wanting to disturb the patient.

"Hi!" Tiffany said.

Mom stirred, but her eyes didn't budge.

Tiffany covered her mouth, realizing her blunder, and motioned for me to follow her out of the room.

"How's she doing?" I asked, gesturing in my mother's direction.

"Huh? Oh, fine. I was wondering if you wanted some coffee." She leaned in conspiratorially, which annoyed me. We weren't close, and I didn't like the implication that we were. "I'm so bored. I'm falling asleep."

Nice, Peter. Real nice gal you snagged this time. I didn't want a coffee. But I did want to get rid of Tiffany for a few moments, so I sent her to get me a chai and a tea for my mom. I stressed that it should be herbal, with no caffeine.

"Sure thing. I'll be back in a jiffy." She smiled at me as if I were a child enjoying a parade. Jesus! Did she even know where she was? I watched her lemon-yellow dress disappear around the corner, listening to the *clip-clop* of her three-inch wedge sandals. Why would anyone wear such preposterous shoes? I half hoped to hear her crashing to the ground.

Back in the room, I settled down in a chair by the bedside—the one Tiffany had just vacated. Mom and I weren't close either, but I still felt I deserved the primo seat in her hospital room.

"Is she gone?" Mom whispered, only one eye open.

"For the moment. She's on a coffee run."

Mom harrumphed.

"How are you feeling?" I stood and bent to take her hand in mine, stopping just before I made an ass out of myself. I pictured her pulling her hand away, like a snapping turtle yanking its head back into its shell.

"I want out of here."

"What did the doctor say? Can you leave soon?" I cursed the hope I could hear in my voice, afraid it would set Mom off.

She waved a bony hand in the air. "Everyone here is an idiot. I feel fine. I want to go home." She pulled her blanket up to her chin, hiding. "I have a nurse at home. She can take care of me."

Not knowing what to say, I went with, "It's nice of Tiffany to keep you company."

Mom rolled her eyes. There was no need to verbalize her thoughts; her body language said it all.

Was it possible that Peter had found a woman who irritated my mother more than I did?

The door sprang open with a bang, and Tiffany appeared. "Goodness, that door is light. I feel like Superman."

For the first time, I noticed her toned arms. Did the woman spend all day in the gym? I wondered if she had a six-pack.

"Oh, you're awake!" Tiffany thrust my chai in my face and then cheerfully presented the tea to my mother, as though offering a diamond ring. "I got you your fave—herbal tea."

I wanted to punch her in the face. I was the one who told her to get the herbal tea, and I was shocked she had managed to remember that for five minutes.

"Thank you," Mom said to me.

Tiffany was too busy being cheerful to notice that my mom had snubbed her. Something gave me the impression she missed a lot of things in life. Had she picked up on the fact that my brother was an arrogant ass who cheated? Maybe it was best if she didn't know.

"So, what did I miss?" Tiffany plunked herself down on the chair opposite me and ripped the cover off her latte, a silly grin spreading over her face.

Mother sipped her tea angrily.

"Tiffany, where did you grow up?" I asked.

"Tie-Fannie," she corrected.

"Yes, I'm sorry." I put my hand up to emphasize my apology. "Where did you grow up?" I didn't bother saying her name correctly. I swore right then and there that I would never call Tiffany by her name ever again; instead, I'd just say, "Hey you."

I enjoyed seeing my mother's scornful frown from behind the cup of herbal tea, mocking the girl.

I should send Peter a thank-you note. Usually, my mother ridiculed me.

"Right here, but I've traveled all over the world."

"Really? Where have you been?"

"So many countries: Mexico, Bermuda, the Caribbean, Puerto Rico, and … Hawaii." She counted each one on her right hand, a glint of pride in her face.

I wanted to correct her, to tell her that Hawaii was actually a part of the States, and that one could make an argument about Puerto Rico, too, even if I was sure the people there felt differently. The puppy dog look on her face told me I'd be wasting my time.

I tried a different approach. "Did Peter take you to these places?"

"Oh no. He's been so busy lately."

I was pretty sure I knew why: he'd been busy avoiding her and being with other women.

"I went to all *those* places for spring break." Tiffany's emphasis was an obvious effort to make herself sound as well traveled as Marco Polo.

"What university did you go to?"

She cocked her head, eying me suspiciously. "College? I didn't go to college."

"Sorry, I just assumed … since you said spring break." A sip of chai helped force my laugh back down my throat. *Where in the world did Peter find this clueless child?*

"My family always goes away each spring. My brothers are in college, so we work around their spring breaks. I considered going to college." She shook her head, giving me the impression she thought it unladylike to seek higher education.

"I see."

I looked to my mother for help, hoping she would say something that might nip all chatter in the bud—she had such a knack for doing that—but instead, she stared at Tiffany with her mouth slightly agape.

"Peter said *you* went to college," she said. Tiffany tried her best to erase the disgust from her face. "And that's why … why you aren't around much." A blush flashed across her face like a lightning bolt.

I could tell she wasn't an experienced liar. It took her some effort to recover from her gaffe. Had Peter told her college turned me into a lesbian? A woman allowed to think for herself apparently led to independence—and lesbianism.

"Yes, I did. I have a PhD in history."

"What's that?"

"A doctorate in history." From the expression on Tiffany's face, I knew I wasn't getting through to her. "I'm a doctor."

"Oh, do you work here?" She waved to the room.

"Nope. Different kind of doctor."

For a brief moment, I got the feeling that my mom was proud of me. Here I was talking to Peter's fiancée, who was dumber than a post, and I could say I was a doctor. Too bad Mom couldn't gloat about this at the club.

"She studies Nazis," Mom offered, her voice betraying no emotion.

Was she proud? Or had I imagined it?

"I've heard of Mengele. Are you a doctor like that?" Tiffany looked hopeful.

Mengele! Did she just ask me if I was a twisted fuck who tortured people in concentration camps?

The blank look on her face suggested she didn't even know it was an insult.

What was it like in her head?

"No. Not at all." I leaned down and pulled a box out of my messenger bag, which sat on the floor. "I got you this, Mom. It's a Kindle. Not only can you read books on it, but you can also listen to books as well." I handed it to her.

A couple of weeks ago, my mother had handed me a note that requested certain titles. I noticed that some of the books were by authors I had already given to her. Sarah and Ethan had done a great job. Her chicken-scratch handwriting was so wobbly and difficult to decipher that, for some reason, it upset me. The fact that it was scrawled with a purple pen disturbed me. Purple and The Scotch-lady? How did I not know she liked purple?

To my surprise, Mom opened the box with a hint of glee. I showed her how to turn the Kindle on. "It's connected to the Internet as well, so you can email and stuff. And when you want to shop"—I pointed to the shop button at the top—"all you have to do is search for any book you want and click buy. It downloads within seconds. It holds hundreds of books." I neglected to tell her that I had my credit card hooked up to her account.

"Hundreds! Who wants to read that many books?" Tiffany slurped her latte. "I tried reading that book everyone was raving about years ago—*Eat, Pray, Live*, or something like that—and couldn't get through the first ten pages. Hundreds?

I don't know if I've met anyone who's read that many books. Even the Julia Roberts movie based on that book bored me." Tiffany snatched the device out of Mom's brittle hands. "Oh, it has apps like my cell phone. Does it have Angry Birds? Now that's something worth having."

Mom cleared her throat and motioned for Tiffany to hand the Kindle back. The clueless woman did not realize that my mother was completely unimpressed with Angry Birds.

Mom turned to me. "Will you read to me, Lizzie?"

"I thought you said that it would read to her," Tiffany said to me. Then turned to Mom. "Why make Lizzie waste her time?"

"Lizzie has a nice reading voice. Must be from all her years teaching at a university." She eyed Tiffany. Was she trying to decide whether Peter's fiancée understood her meaning?

"What would you like me to read?" I asked, trying not to enjoy the moment too much. Maybe I should send Peter a basket of cookies to thank him, not just a card.

"*Eat, Pray, Love,*" snapped my mother.

I busied myself with the Kindle, downloading the book and watching Tiffany out of the corner of my eye. It took her less time to make a decision than I thought it would.

"You know, I told Peter I'd meet him for lunch. I better head out." She threw her purse over her shoulder. She held the door handle and spoke over her shoulder, "Enjoy the book. Um, it's really ... interesting."

And the ditz in yellow was gone.

CHAPTER TEN

A young woman sat at my kitchen table, wide-eyed, while I puttered around getting some snacks ready.

"Would you like something to drink? Tea? Coffee? Water?" I mimed etcetera with my hand.

"Tea would be great." She pulled a couple of notebooks from her over-stuffed backpack.

"Sure, I'll put the kettle on. So, where did you complete your undergrad?" I asked as I filled the kettle.

"University of Puget Sound." She doodled on her notepad, patiently waiting.

Steam spewed out of the kettle, and I lifted it off the burner before it had a chance to scream.

Setting the teacups down, I said, "All right, why don't you tell me about your thesis?"

Hours later, I heard Sarah walk through the front door. "I'm home," she shouted.

"In the kitchen."

My companion looked at her watch. "Goodness! Look at the time." She gathered her notebooks and started to shove them into her bag, struggling to cram everything back in.

"You won't fucking believe what I heard today at work!" Sarah sashayed into the kitchen and then stopped in her tracks. "I'm sorry. I didn't know you had company."

My guest looked nervous, which made me smile. When I was her age, everything made me jumpy. And the first week of the school semester always made me jumpier.

"Sarah, I'd like you to meet Jasmine." I motioned to the awkward but stunning graduate student.

"I've heard all about you." Jasmine put her hand out.

Sarah shook Jasmine's hand as if she wanted to crush it, which surprised me a little. Her eyes suggested she would rather throw the woman out of the house than greet her. Sarah must have had a bad day, I figured, but it was only the third day back after the summer vacation, which didn't bode well for the rest of the year.

Ignoring Sarah for a moment, I turned to Jasmine. "I'll walk you to the door."

My wife followed me so closely I could feel her angry breath on my neck, making Jasmine jumpier. "Call me if you need any help, day or night," I said.

"Thanks," Jasmine said. "Thanks for everything. Nice meeting you, Sarah," she added in a shaky voice.

Sarah popped her head over my shoulder, and Jasmine started as if she'd had a heart attack. "You too, Jas*mine*."

I cringed at Sarah's pronunciation.

After I shut the front door, I turned around to face Sarah. Arms crossed, she was tapping one foot expectantly. "What was that about?" she demanded.

"What was what about: your rudeness to my guest?"

"*My* rudeness?" She placed a hand over her heart. "How would you feel if you walked in while I was entertaining a sexy young woman?"

"Entertaining … ?" I had to laugh. "Sarah—"

"I don't see anything funny about this." Her angry tone increased with each word she spewed.

"What are you insinuating? That I slept with Jasmine and then, just for shits and giggles, made her several cups of tea so she'd still be here when you got home—at your usual time?" I pinned her with a look of disgust. "You think that lowly of me?"

Sarah just grunted. Her scrunched forehead and bunched shoulders suggested she wasn't willing to let the accusation die just yet.

"Tell me, Sarah, what do you think I did?" I bottled up my fury, stopping it from slipping into my tone.

"Jasmine is a very beautiful woman," she sputtered.

"Yes. I'd noticed that." I flashed my "so what?" expression.

Sarah's expression opened out—an aha moment. I could tell she was thinking that if I'd noticed Jasmine's looks, I must have acted on it.

"And so ... that means I fucked her?"

At the word *fuck*, Sarah cringed.

I stormed back into the kitchen to prepare another cup of tea. I didn't really want one, but I needed to stay busy. I didn't want to think. I concentrated on the clicking of the gas burner, and then on the catch of the flame. Next, I grabbed two cups and spooned sugar in each, ignoring Sarah's sugar ban. Not having anything else to do to keep my fingers busy while the water boiled, I started to count to ten.

Sarah watched my every move.

Finally, she said, "Well, why was she here, in *our* home?"

I wasn't ready to let her off the hook yet, even if that little voice in my head said I should.

This isn't worth the fight. Just let it go, Lizzie.

"So, you think that with everything I have going on in my life—my mom, us trying to get pregnant, my research project—you think I have the time, let alone the energy, to have an affair. And you also think I'm either stupid enough or vindictive enough to let you walk in on it." I glared at her, ignoring the whistling kettle; steam rose from it, blurring my vision of Sarah, who stood on the opposite side of the island, near the stovetop.

"You still don't trust me, not after a year of couple's therapy and three years of individual therapy for me."

Sarah sighed, and all the tension left her shoulders. Sadness and guilt filled the void. "Lizzie—"

I put up my hand to silence her words, and then I turned off the burner.

"I'll play by your rules, Sarah. Do you remember Dr. Marcel, my mentor in grad school? That was one of his students. He asked me to help with her dissertation. You do remember Dr. Marcel, don't you? We've had dinner at his home on several occasions. Jasmine is researching growing up in the Third Reich, which happens to be my specialty." Part of me wanted to give my wife a reassuring hug. But the other part felt betrayed. "Did you think ... ?" I couldn't complete my accusation.

Her eyes widened. If we'd been in a cartoon, a light bulb would have gone off over her head. "Oh, I remember you mentioning that." She looked down at the island bench, guiltily. "I didn't expect a history PhD student to be named Jasmine."

"So if she was named Gertrude, you wouldn't have thought I was having an affair?" It was my turn to cross my arms over my chest.

"Not if she looked the exact opposite of Jasmine." Sarah's tone was tinged with culpability, but she flashed an award-winning smile to cover it.

"Jesus, Sarah! I'm not Peter. That girl is just a child. When I first met her, I couldn't help but remember when I started my PhD program. I don't remember being that young, looking that young. And I also thought thank God I'm not anymore. I'm in a much happier place now, here with you."

That softened Sarah up some. "What did she mean when she said she'd heard all about me?"

I huffed, annoyed. "We got to talking about our partners, and how lucky we are that we both have supportive people in our lives. Jasmine's fiancé moved here from Seattle. She was rushing off to be with him."

"Lizzie"—Sarah took my hand in hers—"I'm sorry."

"Maybe I should be flattered that you think I still have enough game for Jasmine." I glanced down at my waistline. With everything going on, although I still took a bike ride each day, it was a short one, not my usual twenty miles. It was definitely showing.

"I'm going to talk to Dr. Marcel," Sarah said, gazing at me hopefully, as though she hoped I'd forgotten what just transpired.

"Really? What do you intend to say: don't accept graduate students who are attractive? I go to universities all of the time to give lectures. Do you think the entire audience is made up of old men in tweed jackets with elbow patches?"

"Yes, that's exactly how I picture it, plus a few old maids."

I rolled my eyes. "Is that how you picture me?"

"On the outside, no. But you can be a bit stuffy."

"I'm meeting Jasmine in two weeks—am I still stuffy?" I couldn't help needling her a little.

"We should have her over for dinner?"

"After your performance today, I doubt she'll want to see you again. Hell, she'll probably cancel on me." I poured hot water into the cups. Sarah didn't ask for tea, but it was my peace offering.

"Good. Mission accomplished," Sarah pouted resolutely.

"I was at Bed Bath & Beyond this morning, would you like to see what I bought?" I wanted to change the subject, knowing it would go nowhere. It was also possible that I wanted to make her feel worse about the situation.

"You went shopping? And at Bed Bath & Beyond?" She pinned me with a skeptical scowl as she added milk to her tea.

"Please don't hint that I was having another liaison. You only get one false accusation per year."

She saluted me. "So, why were you there, then?"

"I had an early lunch with Maddie, and she needed to pop in there for work. I really didn't have a choice."

She nodded, understanding.

I'm not the shopping type. Sarah bought all of my clothes for me during her weekend shopping sprees with her mom. Those two were born shoppers. Me, I despised it.

"Can you stop judging me for one second and follow me?" I led her to our spare bedroom, which we'd planned to turn into a nursery. "Now, I know I probably should have waited for you, but I saw this and I thought it was adorable." The zoo animal wall decals were propped against the far wall. "I haven't put them on yet, but what do you think?"

Sarah put her hand to her mouth. When she could finally speak, she said, "You picked this out ... on your own? Or did Maddie?"

"It was me. If you don't like them, I saved the receipt." I tried to keep the disappointment from my voice.

"Like them ... I love them!"

I grinned. I'd made sure the animals weren't blue or pink, since we didn't know what sex our child would be, and Sarah was adamant about creating a gender-neutral environment. The giraffe, elephant, and hippo were lilac, purple, and aqua respectively. I was disappointed that the decals didn't include an otter.

"Oh, Lizzie. I'm so sorry."

"What do you mean? Won't these work on our walls?" I lifted the packaging to read the instructions.

"Not that. I'm sorry I was so rude to Jasmine. Here you were, shopping for the nursery earlier today."

I smiled and wrapped my arms around her. "You have nothing to worry about, Sarah. But, it does mean you have to take me to dinner to make up for it."

Even though we had a kitchen most chefs would love, we hardly ever cooked. I was home all day, but no one wanted to eat my cooking. Sarah was usually too tired from teaching and coaching to want to cook.

She rested her head against my chest. "It's a deal." She pulled away from me. "But will you still find me attractive when I'm as large as a house?"

"You'll be even more beautiful." I smiled. "Hey, Jasmine mentioned she needed a part-time job. Maybe she can be our nanny," I teased, ducking away carefully so I wouldn't spill my tea when she whacked me in the side.

"Stop hitting me and take me to dinner." I kissed Sarah's forehead. "What happened at work today?"

Her expression clouded over. "I'll tell you over dinner. Okay if Maddie and Doug join us?"

I nodded. "Wow, Doug is like her shadow these days. She never spent that much time with Peter."

"She really likes him. After being with your brother, who was never around, I think she likes being in a real relationship."

"Or she's afraid to let him out of her sight. Are all of you women so mistrustful?"

Sarah didn't dignify that comment with a response. "Go shower. You look like hell."

I laughed. "First you accuse me of having an affair. Now you're telling me I look like hell. You need to make up your mind, missy."

Sarah shucked her skirt and tugged her shirt over her head. She shook her head, tousling her hair, eyes lowered. I eyed her crimson bra and panties.

I started to speak, but her lips were on mine in a shot. Her tongue darted into my mouth, while she peeled my shirt up, pushing away from me briefly to get it off completely. Not wanting to make love to her in the future nursery, I led her to our bedroom, leaving a trail of bras and panties behind us.

We fell on the bed, naked, Sarah's urgency apparent. I eased inside her as she again smothered my mouth with hers. I wasn't sure whether it was her earlier fear, or whether something else had happened, but I sensed Sarah needed to feel sexy, needed me to make love to her. And I was more than willing.

* * *

"It's unlike you to be late." Maddie's mouth curved into a mischievous smile as Sarah and I slid into the booth across from her.

"Hello, troublemaker," I said. I turned to Doug and nodded. He reciprocated.

"Lizzie, you look like hell." Maddie's voice was full of piss and vinegar, but her eyes showed concern.

"Funny, someone else told me that recently." I winked at Sarah. I wanted to add *before seducing me,* but I thought it best to keep that to myself. Maddie was never shy about embarrassing me. Both Sarah and I had showered before leaving the house, but I imagined I could still smell her on my fingers. I brushed my fingertips over my lips, in hope of catching her scent, smiling at the memory.

The waitress appeared to announce the nightly special: steak with blue cheese crumbles. It won me over instantly. Sarah ordered a Caesar salad, which was totally not her norm. I threw her an odd look, but said nothing.

"So, what's this news?" Maddie pounced, as soon as the waitress flipped her notebook shut and padded away on tiny feet. I wondered how the woman stayed erect on such silly looking feet.

I should have known Sarah had called Maddie about whatever the heck happened to her today before she got home. It was highly unusual for her to be so rude to anyone. I still couldn't believe the way she had acted towards Jasmine. As a peace offering, I resolved to call the poor girl in a few days' time and check on her progress in tracking down some of the sources I had suggested.

Sarah sat up straight in her chair and placed both hands on the table. Her posture told me that the news she was about to break was beyond upsetting. "You remember my coworker Jen, who works in the front office?"

Maddie and I nodded. Doug cocked his head in expectation.

"She's bursting out to here"—Sarah indicated extreme

pregnancy—"well, she went home early the other day because she wasn't feeling well." She leaned over the table and whispered, "She surprised her husband—fucking another woman on their couch!"

Maddie covered her mouth. Doug's jaw clenched. He looked like he wanted to punch the husband right in the kisser.

"Can you imagine being seven months pregnant and discovering your husband is having an affair?" Sarah collapsed back into her seat as though she'd been slugged in the face.

"So that's why you accused me of sleeping with Jasmine!" I slapped the table.

Sarah looked away guiltily.

"Who's Jasmine?" Maddie said sourly, staring at me as though she was considering taking me out back and using me as a punching bag. Doug straightened in his seat, too, unsure whether he should wait for my response or be the knight in shining armor.

"Hey now, don't jump to any conclusions like someone else I know." I jerked my head in Sarah's direction. "I'm innocent, I tell you."

Maddie groaned.

"What is that groan supposed to mean?" I was getting pissed all over again.

"Come on, Lizzie. You tried to sleep with me."

And there it was: the elephant in the room that the three of us always avoided. It was the first time any one of us had mentioned it so blatantly in a group setting since it happened. Of course, Sarah and I talked about it in therapy … well, we danced around it, at least.

Doug started to stand, and for a moment I thought he really was going to slug me. Maddie tugged on his arm, forcing him to sit down.

"Thanks for that, Maddie. Much appreciated," I smirked.

"Can someone tell me what's going on?" someone boomed.

I jumped, unused to Doug's voice sounding so manly.

"It happened long ago," Maddie explained.

Doug's jaw kept working. It didn't satisfy him, I could see, and if I were in his shoes, I would want to know all the details as well.

Sarah looked as if she wanted to melt into the cushions of the booth and disappear entirely.

"I made a very stupid mistake—years ago—and I've been living with it ever since."

That got a rise out of Sarah. "Living with it! I never even mention it! I never throw it in your face."

I stared at her. "Until today … "

Doug pinned Maddie with a look that said he wanted answers, right away. "Did you or did you not sleep with Lizzie? And was she dating Sarah at the time?"

I admired his bravery, but his tone was not the way to handle Maddie.

Maddie squared her shoulders, ready for battle. "Excuse me … " She jutted her chin out. "Who in the hell do you think you are?"

"Hold on, everyone!" I snapped my fingers to get them all to look at me. "Let's not drag past mistakes into the present."

"Shut up, Lizzie. I don't want to hear any of your psychobabble—"

"Hey, Lizzie has been making great strides in therapy," Sarah came to my defense.

"Really? Is that why you accused her of fucking someone today?" Maddie somehow managed to eye Sarah while still giving Doug a menacing glance. I wondered if doing that gave her a headache, or eyestrain at the very least.

Diners at surrounding tables stopped talking and turned to stare at our table, some in mid-bite. One older woman left her fork dangling in front of her mouth, watching us intently as if we were a reality television show.

Maddie cleared her throat and stared the woman down

until she looked away.

At that, the other patrons lost interest; out of fear, I guessed.

I turned to Doug. "A few years ago, I was really lost. I know it sounds like a cliché, but I was a total mess. And I made a pass—just a pass—at Maddie. You'll be happy to hear that Maddie slapped my face and told me what she thought of me. I now know that was my way of sabotaging my relationship with Sarah because I was scared to death of settling down. Sarah—" I turned to her, full of remorse—"left me. And it nearly killed me." I could feel my eyes welling up. "Luckily, she was willing to give me another chance, and I will never mess up again." I stared into Sarah's eyes. "Never again."

"Then who's Jasmine?" asked Maddie, not entirely convinced.

"When Sarah came home today, there was a woman in our house."

Maddie scowled.

"She's a PhD student, working with my former mentor, who asked me to meet with her to help her locate sources for her dissertation. Sarah strutted in, saw me talking with a beautiful young woman, and assumed the worst."

Sarah smiled sheepishly. "In my defense, Jasmine is hot as shit."

I shrugged, conceding the point. "And she's engaged. How did you not notice the huge diamond on her finger? It's bigger than yours." I pointed to Sarah's ring finger.

Maddie pulled her cell phone out of her back jeans pocket. "What's her last name?"

"No idea. Why?"

"I'm looking her up." Her crinkled brow said *duh*.

"Can't be too many PhD candidates named Jasmine on the school's website."

Maddie snapped her fingers. "Good thinking!" Several seconds later, she uttered, "Whoa!"

Doug whipped the phone away from her and held it in front of his face. He briefly flashed me a look that was all conquering hero.

"You see!" declared Sarah.

Doug and Maddie both nodded.

"So, Maddie, if you came home and Doug was sitting down having tea with Jasmine, would your first thought be, 'That bastard!'"

Doug leaned closer to Maddie, eyebrows raised.

"Here ya go," the waitress interrupted. She plunked her tray down on a stand her coworker had set up and started to dish out the meals.

"Ha! Saved by steak." I winked at Maddie.

Doug's determined smile suggested he'd get his answer later that night anyway.

CHAPTER ELEVEN

Summer passed quickly, and I stepped out of my house one morning to find myself shocked by the crisp fall air. How had I missed an entire season? Not once had Sarah and I ventured out to our cabin in Idaho. Usually, we spent several summer weeks up there during her school break. My thirty-first birthday slipped by almost unnoticed by me.

With fall came another check-up for Mom. Once again, I found myself waiting in the oncologist's office while my mother was in the back, hopefully hearing encouraging news—not that I ever knew what was said. Usually, my stony-faced mother sauntered out from behind the door and then strode right for the exit. She didn't even bother saying my name or anything. I had to keep an eye out for her, bolting up as soon as I caught a glimpse of her navy suit whisking by.

This time, I saw the door open slightly. A pause. Maybe the person behind the door had dropped something and leaned down to get it, or maybe a nurse had called out to the patient to say something. Or maybe someone just wasn't ready to face the world outside yet.

Filled with dread, I couldn't take my eyes off the door. Then it opened forcefully and an elderly gentleman ambled out, heading straight for the exit. He looked defeated. I'm not the religious type, but I said a small prayer for him. A woman followed him, moving as though the world was rubble around her feet. *Which one received the news?* I wondered.

I sat there, contemplating what would be harder: hearing that I had cancer or hearing that Sarah did? Actually, that was a no-brainer. I would never want Sarah to suffer. I said another prayer. *If one of us is struck, let it be me.*

Finally, my frail mother appeared. This time, she paused and stared at me, her face slack with an expression I couldn't make out. She flashed the tiniest of smiles. And then— poof!—it was gone. I wondered if I imagined it in the first place. Mom marched to the exit, and I followed dutifully, feeling slightly relieved.

When I dropped her off at her house, she mentioned that my dad would be away on business over the weekend.

"If you don't have plans, why don't you come by on Saturday, for lunch? Bring that girl with you."

Before I could answer yes or no, Mom pranced up the staircase to her front door, moving with a lightness I had never seen before.

That girl. My wife.

I wasn't sure whether to be angry or happy. It was the first time Mom had ever asked any of my partners over. Sarah had been to my brother's house on a few occasions, but she had never set foot in my parents' home.

That girl!

I started laughing so hard I had to pull off the highway. Then, inexplicably, tears started falling from my eyes. Something told me Mom's smile wasn't one of victory, but of relief.

Was it over?

And if it was, what: the battle, or the treatments?

* * *

Ever since we'd bought our house, I'd spent most of my days in my office, which doubled as the library. When we started house hunting for the second time, after Sarah forgave me, I took it more seriously than the first. Before the whole Maddie situation, Sarah had wanted us to buy a house, but I was too chickenshit to tell her I wasn't ready to take that step. Instead, every time we went looking, I found something wrong with the house. Sarah had assumed I was being overly picky because I wanted our house to be perfect.

When we officially began looking the second time, I had a different goal: to rein in Sarah's desire to spend money, too much money. Yes, we both had trust funds, but I didn't think we should spend willy-nilly. I wanted a relatively small home with no extra bedrooms. Guest bedrooms invited visitors, and I liked my space. Sarah said she agreed, so the first couple of weeks we saw only average-sized homes.

Then I noticed something. Sarah kept inviting me to used bookstores with her, helping me track down wonderful leather-bound editions of classics.

Her explanation was simple, "We can't have a house filled with just Nazi books. The first time I visited your apartment I was terrified by all the swastikas on the shelves. I thought I'd walked into some type of serial-killer trap."

I laughed. "Occupational hazard, I guess."

She had placed a loving hand on my shoulder. "We don't want people thinking you're a Neo-Nazi *and* socially awkward."

"So, just socially awkward is okay?" I asked.

"Not much I can change about that. It is your personality," she retorted, with a wink.

At first, I loved the shopping excursions, which was saying a lot, since I loathed shopping. Then I noticed a second trend. The more books we bought, the bigger the houses we visited. At first they weren't substantially larger, but they gradually started getting out of my comfort zone. Each time, Sarah found something wrong with the house.

My gut told me I was being played, but I couldn't put my finger on how. This continued for a few months. We bought more and more books, and the houses we toured were bigger and bigger.

One Monday morning, while she was getting ready for work, Sarah mentioned that the agent had a home she wanted to show us that evening. "She says it's perfect for us."

I tried not to roll my eyes. Our agent said that every time. "Sure, I'll meet you there."

The house was a mansion. Well, not really, but it was much too large for my taste. When I pulled up at the address, I doubled-checked Sarah's handwritten note with the address on the side of the home.

"She's out of her frigging mind," I grumbled when I opened my car door to greet Sarah and the agent on the stoop. The house was near the old town section of Fort Collins. It wasn't new, but nor was it as old as some in the area.

I wanted a new home; the idea of living in a place that other people had once lived in creeped me out. What could I say? I was both a neat freak and a control freak.

Sarah rushed up to me and threw her arms around my neck, giving me a peck on the cheek. "Isn't this beautiful?" she squealed in delight.

I grinned, knowing she was playacting for my benefit, to lure me in.

The agent walked us around the house. I had to agree it was lovely. The floor plan was open—I hated tight spaces—with four bedrooms. I cringed at the thought of people staying in our house and having to act happy to have them. Acting jubilant was not my forte.

But this time, Sarah wasn't finding fault with the home. As we neared the end of the tour, I wasn't yet sold. But I knew Sarah was. I was mentally preparing for battle.

We don't need this much space for the two of us, I kept thinking. *Too large. Too expensive. And much too pretentious.*

"There's one last room I want to show you two, especially you, Lizzie," said the agent.

I raised an eyebrow, curious.

She opened the door to the library. I kid you not, it was the one I had always dreamed of. Floor-to-ceiling bookshelves, with a few of the quaint little ladders I always found so charming. At the far end, bay windows presented a wonderful view of the foothills. And the room was big enough to accommodate a massive desk, a couch, and leather reading chairs, all without feeling cramped. Hell, I could put a pool table off to the side if I wanted to. Maybe even a Ping-Pong table.

My mouth hit the floor. Sarah and the agent stared at me, waiting.

"How long have you been holding out?" I asked Sarah.

She shrugged and gave me an unconvincing, "I don't know what you mean" look.

I crossed my arms.

Sarah put her palms up. "All right. Mom and I found it weeks ago."

"You played me." I walked to the windows and looked out, keeping my back to both of them.

"What do you think?" asked the agent.

Without turning around, I said, "Where do I sign?"

Sarah let out a relieved squawk and rushed toward me, almost slamming me against the windows as she enveloped me in her arms.

"Nicely played."

She giggled. "Now you have a place for all those books," she whispered.

I nodded. "You aren't getting out of it. We still have plenty of space to fill. Our book shopping trips aren't over just because you got your way."

"Deal." She squeezed me tight. "Maddie's going to be thrilled!"

"I take it she's already seen it."

"Of course. We can't buy a place without our designer's approval." Sarah whisked a strand of hair out of her face, triumphantly.

"I'm surprised you didn't just go ahead and buy it."

"Don't be silly. Your input is important to me." She almost looked sincere. "Plus, I can't forge your signature."

Sarah found me in my office, snapping me back to reality. "There you are?"

I looked up from my gin and tonic, leaving the memories in the past.

"Why are you sitting in the dark?" I didn't hear a hint of accusation in her tone, only concern.

I sighed. "I don't know, really."

Since leaving Mom earlier that day, I couldn't get the thought out of my head that it was over. Just when I was finally getting through to her, it was over. For thirty years that woman had ignored me or tortured me. And then, for a few months, I had a mother, albeit one still completely on her terms.

Sarah flicked on the desk lamp. I hadn't realized that the sun had gone down, and I was sitting in the dark. She left the room and soon returned with a glass of wine. Perching on the leather chair next to mine, she said, "Do you want to talk about it?" Then she took a nervous sip of wine.

She sniffed loudly and I watched her light a Yankee Candle.

Knowing Sarah wouldn't let her question fade away like the smoke from the candle, I finally answered, "Not much to talk about really. I don't know what's going on."

"With your mom?"

I let out a sad laugh, "with anything." I walked to the small bar in my office and replenished my drink, heavy on the gin. My back to Sarah, I asked, "Why do we crave love from those who are most incapable of loving?"

I heard the creak of leather as Sarah stood. Wrapping her arms around my waist, she gave me a squeeze. "Nothing about love is easy."

"Then why do we crave it so much?" I stifled a sob.

As always, Sarah was in tune with my thoughts. "Just enjoy the time you have left with her, Lizzie. This is your one chance. Take it."

I broke free from her arms and slumped against the bar. "Do you know she's never told me that she loves me? Not once."

"Have you told her that?"

I shook my head. "It would mean nothing to her."

"That may be true, but would it mean something to you?"

CHAPTER TWELVE

As Sarah and I approached my parents' front door, I couldn't shake the odd feeling in the pit of my stomach. For years I couldn't wait to leave this place and never return. I wouldn't say my childhood was dreadful; after all, some adults have painful childhood memories such as sexual or physical abuse, or both. Me, I had just grown up knowing I didn't matter to anyone in my family. It sounded like a pathetic complaint. Did I really need my parents to give me a hug and say, "I love you" every day? Was I that needy, that fucking weak?

Simply put: yes.

My mother was never the loving type. Hugs were out of the question. She acted more like a drill sergeant toughening me up for war. It was difficult in the earlier years, as I was a sensitive child. Later on, when I outed myself, it became much worse. She became worse. She no longer tried to toughen me up for battle; instead, she declared war on me.

For years I tried to believe my childhood didn't affect me. I was stronger than that. Independent. Too intelligent to let something so frivolous bother me. I studied Nazis, for Christ's sake. I had read countless stories about people who really lived through hell, stuff that no one could possibly imagine, let alone survive—yet many did.

Why was I letting my parents, especially my mother's

lack of feeling, destroy me? Pathetic. I felt feeble. So I pushed it down. All those feelings, or lack thereof, I discounted completely. I told myself not to be a fool. *Push through it. People have lived through much worse. Get the fuck over yourself, Lizzie.*

Then I almost lost Sarah through not dealing with my childhood, through lying to myself that I was okay, that I didn't need anyone to complete me.

My therapist pointed that out right from the start. She asked me if I found it interesting that my research centered on children of the Third Reich. Many of the young boys who belonged to the Hitler Youth were shipped off, isolated from parental influence. Many more were orphaned at a young age. Why was I so fascinated by a generation that had grown up without parents?

I felt like a fucking idiot. The answer was staring me in the face the entire time, yet I never saw it. I could have studied so many different aspects of World War II, but this was the one that pulled me in.

Now Sarah and I wanted to bring our own child into the world at the same time that I was preparing to say good-bye to my uncaring mother. Talk about conflicting emotions. But Sarah was right: I needed to make peace with my mom, The Scotch-lady. If I didn't, I might never be completely whole.

Sarah gave my hand a squeeze before she reached out to ring the bell.

Tiffany opened the door. Shit!

I guess today wasn't the day to have my reckoning.

"Hello, there. We keep bumping into each other." She giggled like a vapid schoolgirl.

"Is Peter here?" asked Sarah. She gave me an "I'm sorry" look, since she knew I wanted this day to be just the three of us.

Tiffany marched off toward the main part of the house, answering over her shoulder, "Nope. He dropped me off on his way to golf." She paused and whispered conspiratorially, "He didn't want your mom to be alone."

"Peter sure has been playing a lot of golf lately."

Did Tiffany know that Peter wasn't really a sports guy? I was positive he played the occasional round of golf for business purposes, but every weekend? No way.

"He's become quite the fanatic," Mom said from her leather throne in the front room. Her beady eyes glinted. I knew she was thinking the same thought as me. Was that why she wasn't as close to her firstborn these days? Before Maddie left my brother at the altar, my mother had favored Peter. Did she know why Maddie had flown the coop? Maybe she read Maddie's note, pinned to the wedding dress: "Give it to her." Had it dawned on Mom that Peter had grown to be just like her husband?

I learned late in the game that my father had kept a woman on the side for years. My mother knew all along, but she looked the other way. Was she angry with Peter? Disappointed? Disgusted? Or angry with herself for not leaving my father?

Quite possibly, she just hated Tiffany.

I wasn't a fan either. I could live with the fact that Tiffany was not the brightest, but her flippant attitude grated on my nerves. Like her comment, "We keep running into each other." My fucking mother was dying, you dingbat.

Could I be jealous of Tiffany? Here she was, engaged to a man who couldn't keep his pants on and being dropped off to keep her future mother-in-law (who despised her) company, and yet she acted like it was a day at Disneyland.

No. I couldn't live that way. As much as my mind tortured me, I did appreciate I wasn't a Stepford Wife. And I wasn't married to one either.

"How are you feeling, Evelyn?" asked Sarah.

Mom set her Kindle aside. I smiled that she was actually using it.

"I'm not dead yet, although I think some treat me like I am."

Was that a dig at Peter?

Years ago, I would have loved to hear her take a jab at my brother. The once-mighty Peter had fallen. Today, seeing her thin body engulfed by an afghan in her massive leather chair, it was disconcerting.

Sarah didn't respond, just nodded sympathetically. What could one say to that?

"You," my mother stretched out a bony finger in Tiffany's direction, "get me a tea," she barked.

Tiffany smiled, as if someone just handed her some cotton candy, and bounded into the kitchen.

I watched, amazed—or at least overly inquisitive. I followed Tiffany into the kitchen on the pretense of making drinks for Sarah and myself. My real goal was to see if Tiffany still wore her happy face.

Much to my consternation, she did. Where had Peter found such a lobotomized woman?

"So, how are things?" I purposefully didn't say her name, since I couldn't bring myself to pronounce it her way. Maybe I should tell her that my name was pronounced Lizz-Aye.

"Fantastic. You?" She plopped a tea bag into a Wedgewood teacup.

I nodded, dumbfounded. "Have you and Peter set a date for the wedding?"

"December twenty-fifth." She set the cream and sugar on a tray.

Tiffany rattled off the date as if she had no clue that date held any other significance. Was she Jewish?

"Christmas, huh? I wouldn't have guessed that."

Peter had scheduled his first wedding on my birthday. He always had to be the center of attention, which made his absences lately decidedly odd. Had he realized he couldn't compete with a woman with cancer?

"Peter says work is slower at that time of year."

So that was it: it was more convenient for him, even if not for the rest of the world.

"We're going to Fiji for our honeymoon. Peter says it'll

be warm, but I'm really worried. Won't it be cold in the winter?" For the first time, I noticed a different emotion on her face: concern.

"I think Peter's right. That's their summer."

"What?"

I imagined the concept bouncing around frantically inside her empty head, searching for an anchor.

"It's on the other side of the world. When we have winter, they have summer."

"Really? Who would have thought that?" Joy returned to her eyes.

"Would you like a drink?" I asked, hoping to bury this inane conversation before I insulted her.

"Wine would be great."

I looked at the clock on the microwave. 11:15 a.m. Interesting. Maybe she hadn't had a lobotomy after all.

"Red or white?" I asked, heading for my parents' wine cellar.

She crinkled her brow. "Makes no difference to me."

I was sure it didn't. And neither did anything else. Except for cold weather on her honeymoon.

An hour later, the four of us sat around the table, eating lunch. Tiffany was on her third glass of wine, but she didn't seem overly tipsy. Hard to tell with her, though. What qualified as tipsy and what was just ignorance?

"Evelyn, where did you and Charles go for your honeymoon?" Tiffany said it like she expected some epic adventure.

"Yellowstone," my mom snapped. She stirred some pasta salad around on her plate. I don't think I'd seen her actually eat one morsel of food.

"Where's that?"

I could see Tiffany still expected something luxurious.

My mom looked up from her plate and then back down.

"It's in Wyoming, mostly," I answered for her. "Part of the park is in Montana—where my parents are from."

"Park?" Tiffany's expectations were dropping drastically by the second, and so was her smile.

"It's a national park. When my parents married, my dad was just starting out," I explained. Had Peter claimed we were from old money, that his ancestors were robber barons and his father struck out West to make a name for himself? Did Tiffany know that my parents had lived in a trailer home at one point? I doubt it. Mom was usually desperate to keep all the cool aspects about them under wraps.

"Oh," she sounded beyond disappointed.

To help cheer Tiffany up, I turned to Sarah. "They're going to Fiji for their honeymoon."

Sarah picked up on my motive. "Oh, that sounds romantic. Have you set a date?"

I braced for Sarah's reaction.

"December twenty-fifth." This time, Tiffany eyed me cautiously.

"Christmas! And then Fiji for the New Year. That's wonderful."

Tiffany seemed relieved to find that Sarah's reaction was the polar opposite of mine.

"Marriage is like prostitution," said my mother.

The entire mood at the table slid into a black hole. I had been trying to keep it at even keel, but after that declaration, I was clueless how to yank it back from the brink of complete disaster.

Sarah and I both knew not to react to Mom's statement; that was what she wanted.

Tiffany, however, took the bait. "What do you mean, Evelyn?" she asked.

I really didn't want Mom to elaborate.

"The only reason men marry is because it's good for their careers. They don't love anyone. They put a ring on your finger to take you off the market. Marking their territory. Then they come and go as they please. And if you want anything, you better be willing to spread them." Mom dropped her fork onto her plate. Over the clattering sound, she uttered, "Golf. You think Peter's playing golf today? And Charles is away on business? Please. Marriage is legalized prostitution. You may feel respectable, but no wife is. You might as well get used to it or leave like—"

Tiffany took a healthy slug of her wine. Her body language suggested she knew all along why Peter was absent. Was she playacting the ditz as a cover, a coping mechanism? Shit. I felt horrible. Was she just subscribing to a role Peter defined for her? It would be the type of wife he wanted, after the Maddie debacle: a woman who wouldn't challenge him. Someone who would just be beautiful and not expect too much from him, or from the marriage.

I let out a long breath.

A cloud re-emerged over Tiffany's demeanor, but she plastered another fake smile on her face. I wanted to tell her to stop, that it wasn't worth it. Financial security wasn't worth it. If she didn't believe me, take a look across the table. Look at my mom. Really look at her. Was that what Tiffany wanted out of life?

"You two,"—Mom pointed at Sarah and me—"do either of you play *golf,* eh?" She started to cackle, but it turned into a coughing fit.

Neither of us responded.

"That's one thing about Lizzie—she's never cared about what others think. It used to drive me fucking crazy, but now …" Mom rose slowly to her feet. After she steadied herself, she announced, "I'm tired. I'm going to take a nap."

When she was out of earshot, Sarah rose to clear the dishes. At first, I was too thunderstruck to move. Did my mom just compliment me in some weird way? Or was that another veiled insult?

Tiffany filled her wineglass again. She must have seen me eye her brimming glass. "I have to wait for Peter to pick me up. My car is in the shop," she said, clearing her throat.

"Would you like me to drive you home?" I offered.

"Does he still live on Quentin?" It wasn't until I asked the question that I realized how ridiculous it sounded. I didn't know where my brother lived, and he didn't know where I lived. God, we were a fucked up family! How did I think I would ever get some type of closure?

"No, he moved after ..." It didn't seem like she'd run out of words, just that she was defeated. She had run out of desire. "I should help Sarah." She hopped up, shaking her head from either standing too quickly or from the copious amount of wine she had consumed. My money was on the wine.

"How you doing?" asked Sarah on the drive back to Fort Collins.

I shook my head and gripped the steering wheel. "What an awful afternoon."

We drove in silence for a few minutes. Then I broke it. "I feel terrible for Tiffany. Is it all an act?"

"I think so. She's so young, and Peter ... "

"Why does my family chew everyone up and spit them out?"

Speechless, Sarah patted my leg.

"And to watch my mom dig her claws into Tiffany. At first I was thrilled I wasn't the target, but shit, this is worse. I can at least stand up to her. Do you think Peter ever felt this way? Conflicted about not being the target, but feeling bad for me?"

She avoided answering, instead saying, "What do you think?"

"Not a chance in hell. Peter's too much like them, or like my mother at least. To be honest, Sarah, this whole experience is showing me just how much I don't know my father. The man is either mute or not present. How does he feel? Mom is bitter. Beyond bitter. But is he? For the life of me, I can't figure out why they never divorced. For as long as I remember, they've always been like that, always combative.

What kind of life is that?"

* * *

Two days later, I received an email from my father requesting my presence at dinner. The message didn't say much, but I formed the impression it would be just the two of us. We met at the same restaurant.

Once again, I found my father sitting in the dark, stylish bar in an overstuffed leather chair. He swirled a bourbon, but didn't seem to be drinking. I watched him briefly as he stared blankly out of the window. He didn't move, speak, drink, or anything. It was the saddest I had ever seen him.

"Hello," I said, taking a seat across from him.

He nodded and motioned for the waitress to approach.

"What'll ya have, darling?" Her bouncy attitude didn't fit my father's somber mood.

"Gin and tonic. Double please."

I had prepared ahead of time, so that Sarah and Maddie were in a different restaurant nearby, waiting to take me home. No one said it out loud, but I think we all sensed what was about to happen.

Mom's chemo treatment had ended abruptly. Just yesterday, when I arrived to pick her up, she announced that she wasn't going. Not that day. Not ever. And with that, she'd shooed me away.

"Lizzie ... " My father sipped his bourbon. "Your mom has decided to stop her treatment. The last test revealed that it wasn't working and—"

"Here ya go." The bubbly waitress appeared. "One G and T, heavy on the G." She plopped the drink down and rushed off, smiling.

I held the glass, watching condensation slide down onto my fingers before dripping onto the arm of the chair. "I see," I finally said.

"We knew that it was a long shot. It was caught so late ... "

A long shot. It seemed cruel to refer to someone's life as a long shot, but oddly fitting, too. Mom was always playing games. Until recently, it looked like she'd win by playing dirty. Cancer—the great equalizer. Rich, poor, happy, or sad, it didn't matter. Cancer struck and left death and destruction in its wake.

I let out a long breath and swallowed a mouthful of my drink in an attempt to force my emotions back. I needed to hold on. There would be time for me to fall apart—later, not now. I had to be strong.

Neither of us spoke.

"Another round?" The waitress came by again. My father and I nodded gravely. Our mood finally seeped into hers, and she hurried away less cheerfully this time.

"Is there anything that can be done to make her more comfortable?" I asked.

"I've called Hospice. They'll work with your mom's nurse, make sure she has OxyContin and morphine to ease the pain. She wants everything to be on her terms, like normal." For the first time, I saw a slight smile cross his lips.

"What was she like, when you met her?" The question popped out of my mouth before I could stop it; even I was floored by it.

Dad cradled his tumbler with both hands and stared into his lap. "Strong, determined, not as harsh. The more successful we became, the more her fear took over. She never wanted to return to where we started. Power. She craved power. I loved your mother once, Lizzie." He lifted his haggard face to gaze into my eyes. "Until she stopped letting me."

Dad excused himself, and ambled to the bathroom, looking like an old man. I sat in my chair, stunned, unable to think of what I should do or say.

When he returned, my father asked, "Do you have a ride home?"

"Yeah." I nodded to ensure my meaning got across. I

wasn't sure he had heard me; my voice felt stuck in the back of my throat.

He placed a hand on my shoulder. "She would like you to continue visiting," he said, and then he was gone. I guess he had opted not to have dinner, and I wasn't hungry now either.

I flagged the waitress, cancelled the second round, and asked her to settle the bill.

She waved me off. "I'll just put it on Mr. Petrie's tab, honey."

My drink was still two-thirds full. It took me more than an hour to finish it. Tempted to order another, I fished my phone out before I slipped into a miasma I couldn't recover from. Maddie and Sarah rushed inside to retrieve me.

I gazed into Sarah's eyes and whispered, "He loved her … in another lifetime."

Past tense. Soon, she would always be in the past tense. It was over. The drill sergeant had lost this battle, and consequently, the war.

Cancer was unforgiving. It didn't care about power. It crushed Mom like a bug smashed into a windshield, only not as quickly. It teased her with the hope of beating it.

CHAPTER THIRTEEN

Sarah and I sat in the doctor's consultation room to discuss our future *test-tube baby*—a phrase Sarah forbade me from uttering out loud. She preferred the clinical in vitro fertilization or IVF. Personally, when I heard it put that way, I started to freak out.

The room wasn't overly clinical. A vase with fresh daisies sat on the far table. The wall behind displayed photos of smiling babies and cooing parents. The colors were soothing. Everything seemed purposefully cheerful, except for the schematic of the IVF process; it reminded me of those silly cartoons they showed in elementary school, explaining how a bill was turned into a law. The drawing in the office wasn't very cheerful either. It depicted a female form with a red spot marking her reproductive parts and an arrow pointing to a laboratory dish. I stopped inspecting it even before it detailed two other steps in the process.

I always cringed whenever I saw or thought of a Petri dish. Having the surname Petrie didn't help. I felt like a science experiment, akin to Harry Harlow's experiments on baby monkeys raised by unfeeling mothers.

I took a deep breath in an attempt to calm myself. It didn't work. I was certain Sarah could see my heart pumping inside my chest, so hard I thought for sure it was heaving up and down like an overwrought piston about to explode.

The doctor sat in a chair behind the desk. She had a kind face and appeared to be in her late forties. She in no way resembled a mad scientist, much to my chagrin.

"So, Sarah and Lizzie, I understand you would like to extract eggs from Lizzie, and then you, Sarah, will carry the baby. Is that correct?" Her soft voice matched her caring appearance.

Extract—the word made me shudder.

"That's correct," said Sarah, our unofficial spokesperson.

The doctor jotted something on a notepad before stating, "Wonderful. The process has really advanced since it was first accomplished in 1978."

My brain focused on the year. I hadn't considered researching the history of test-tube babies.

Realizing the woman was still speaking, I checked back into the conversation. "We'll need to chart Lizzie's cycle, and then stimulate her ovulatory process and remove ova, or eggs, from her ovaries. We'll then add sperm to fertilize them in a laboratory. The zygote ... " She paused and looked directly at me. I didn't like her assumption that I was clueless about the process, even though I was. "The fertilized egg is cultured for two to six days, and then we'll implant it into Sarah's uterus."

All the words: *ovulatory, ova, zygote, sperm*, and *uterus* bounced around in my head like an out-of-control Ping-Pong ball. The woman was a mad scientist after all. But she was even scarier for looking so unassuming.

Sarah reached for my hand. "How do you extract Lizzie's eggs?"

I could have done without that question. Ignorance is bliss.

Dr. Frankenstein gazed at me sweetly, and replied, "We use a transvaginal technique called transvaginal oocyte retrieval."

I wanted to say, "Come again."

She must have sensed that all I heard was jibberish.

"Basically, it involves using a needle to pierce the vaginal wall to get to your ovaries."

I honed in on two words: *needle* and *pierce*.

Sarah squeezed my hand tighter. I would have squeezed back if I wasn't mortified by this sweet woman calmly talking about torturing me with modern-day medicine.

The nut job continued. "Lizzie will be given drugs that will stimulate her ovaries, with the hope that she'll produce several eggs."

I no longer liked the term test-tube baby. And I wasn't fond of IVF either. The cheerful consultation room suddenly felt like a prison, and I felt like a prisoner undergoing outrageous and painful medical tortures, all for the glory of a mad scientist.

If Sarah hadn't had a vise-like grip on my hand, I would have bolted.

"However, quality eggs are still the goal, not necessarily quantity."

So, I wasn't exactly a factory egg producer but more of a free-range chicken.

I didn't look at Sarah or the doctor so my true feelings would remain undetected.

Panic.

I was panicking. All of this was becoming real to me. Soon, I'd be taking egg-inducing drugs and then this crazy woman was going to insert a needle into me to suck them out.

What the fucking hell?

Who in the fuck thought of this?

Any desire I had to research test-tube babies oozed out of me. I imagined seeing a puddle of fear forming around my feet.

By some miracle, I managed to remain quiet for the rest of the appointment. The doctor kept asking Sarah all the questions, like what would we do with the extra eggs: freeze them, or donate them?

The longer we stayed, the more determined I became to

never eat another egg in all my life. This whole stealing of eggs was barbaric.

Dates were discussed. Soon, Sarah was standing and shaking the loon's hand saying, "Thank you so much for meeting us. You have been so reassuring, and I know I speak for both of us when I say we are thrilled to be starting this process."

The doctor smiled. I reached down deep inside to yank a smile out. I imagined I was pulling a string connected to the sun on the other side of the earth and forcing its warmth and radiance to appear hours before the dawn.

We made it to the parking lot before Sarah noticed my dazed look. When she plucked the keys out of my hand, I didn't even protest. Our appointment was early in the day, so Sarah had taken the rest of the day off.

It wasn't until we'd been driving for well over forty minutes that I realized we weren't heading home. Instead, we were driving through Estes Park, a small town outside the entrance of Rocky Mountain National Park.

"Are we going hiking?" I asked.

"Not really. We're meeting Maddie and Doug for lunch, and then hopefully we'll explore a bit. Do you know what season this is?"

"Fall," I said with no confidence it was the correct answer.

"True, and it's elk-rutting season."

I rubbed my eyes and swallowed. "What are you talking about?"

"Large numbers of elk gather together and you can hear the sounds of the bulls bugling. Rocky Mountain National Park has more elk than Yellowstone."

"Why?"

"Fewer wolves and grizzly bears," she said matter-of-factly as she pulled off the main street to park the car in the public lot.

We met Maddie and Doug at a small sandwich shop that

had a view of Main Street. The place was atypical for Sarah and Maddie. The plastic chairs and cheap tables covered with red-and-white checkered tablecloths made me question why we were eating here.

I must have looked rattled, because Maddie was on her best behavior for once. She didn't crack any jokes at my expense. Normally, I would have minded being handled with kid gloves, but I didn't think I could handle too much joviality today.

"This place has the best meatball subs," said Doug.

It was Doug's place; that explained the décor.

"So Lizzie," he continued, "are you ready to hear the elk bugling? They say it's one of the most unique sounds in nature, like the howl of a wolf."

"Sounds great," I replied not so enthusiastically.

Maddie offered Doug a sweet smile. "Don't worry, sweetheart. I think Lizzie's still in shock from her appointment."

Doug nodded sympathetically.

Sarah's warm hand slipped onto my thigh. "The poor thing had to sit there and listen to words like zygote, sperm, and ova—" Sarah burst into laughter.

"Hey! They're going to stick a needle in me and suck my eggs out," I pouted.

"And Sarah's going to carry the baby and then go through this thing called birth." Maddie arched her eyebrows, clearly curious as to how I would respond.

I didn't.

Just then, I saw a person bolt past the window. Followed by two more. They didn't seem like they were running to catch a bus or something. They were sprinting for their lives. I pointed out the window, speechless.

Everyone looked in time to see a massive elk charging after the runners.

Then I heard the sound. The bull screamed.

"Shit," muttered Doug. "I wish people would respect elk

more, especially during rutting season. Those people probably called out to get a better photo or something." He shook his head in dismay.

I had been to Estes countless times, but I had never seen elk roaming through the town. It was like a mini elk apocalypse outside, and we had front-row seats.

"Shall I order the meatball subs?" asked Maddie. Without waiting for our answers, she headed for the cash register.

"This is insane." Sarah's mouth was slightly agape as she watched the madness outside.

Doug agreed. "The males are very combative right now." He turned to me. "Do you know that their urethras point upward, so when they piss it shoots onto their hide? The females are attracted to the scent."

Maddie returned just in time to hear his disgusting tidbit. "You see, Lizzie. You thought you had it bad. At least you don't have to pee on yourself."

Everyone got a kick out of that, and I had to admit that, for the first time that day, I felt relieved. Despite all the mayhem taking place outside, sitting inside with Sarah and our friends and sharing lunch had turned it into a normal day— for me, at least, if not for the people being chased.

"So, tell me, who came up with this idea for today?" I stared directly at Maddie.

Her guilty smile answered me.

"Her first suggestion was taking you to eat Rocky Mountain oysters," said Doug.

My mouth fell open. "Fried cow balls. You wanted me to eat fried cow balls?"

She shrugged. "I thought it was kinda fitting, considering."

I couldn't help but laugh.

CHAPTER FOURTEEN

At the start of November, Sarah surprised me by taking me to Breckenridge for a weekend. The winter tourists hadn't yet arrived in full force. We were sitting in a restaurant next to a roaring fire, Sarah looking radiant in a Norwegian ski sweater she had purchased specifically for the getaway. Neither of us planned to ski because there wasn't much snow to speak of and I had never skied in my life, but Sarah hardly ever missed a chance to shop.

"You're quiet over there," she said, washing the words away with a sip of water, cautious doe eyes gazing at me over the rim.

I smiled awkwardly. "I'm sorry. You take me away on a romantic getaway, and here I am ruminating."

"This doesn't have to be a romantic getaway, Lizzie. I just thought it'd be good for you to get away from everything for a couple of days. Relax, have a little fun, eat some good food." She motioned to the steak that sat untouched on my plate.

Usually, I inhaled every meal that was placed before me. Today, not even a steak could tempt me.

"I'm worried about you." Her voice was soft, supportive. "I don't know how I would handle my mother dying, and your situation has added layers of difficulty."

"'Added layers of difficulty,'" I repeated. "That's an understatement." I sliced off a small piece of steak—for her benefit, not because I was hungry. "I've been reading, I think we should go organic, for the baby's sake."

Sarah set down her water glass, taken aback by the sudden change of topic. Her eyebrows shot up.

"I just think fewer pesticides and other chemicals would be better for us, and for the baby," I continued. "I've been living with an illness that many people believe has environmental causes. And cancer ... well ... I just think it would be better. Safer." I looked away, feeling foolish. I wasn't the type to support organic food or to change my diet because it was trendy.

"Wow. I don't know whether I should be impressed or check to see if you have a fever," Sarah teased. "Have you considered veganism?"

I had to laugh. "Don't push your luck. Buying organic will be a huge step for me."

"What other changes do you want to make?"

I scrunched up my forehead, thinking. "I don't know. Let me do some more research."

"You're going to be one of *those* parents, aren't you?" She looked amused, albeit slightly concerned.

"What do you mean, 'one of those'?" I crossed my arms, playfully. It felt good to banter back and forth.

"The type who tries new fads. Certain toys, music ..." She motioned a never-ending cycle.

"Maybe," I admitted. "I just want ... I want our child to have what I didn't."

She leaned closer to me. "Which is what?"

"To feel loved. To have options."

A tear formed in the corner of her eye. I reached over and wiped it away with a fingertip.

"You never fail to surprise me," she said.

"Hopefully in a good way."

"At least forty percent of the time."

I chuckled. "Forty! That's harsh!"

"Honesty hurts."

I waved her words away. "I bet our kid will be smarter than Ethan's."

Sarah shook her head and tsked. "Don't even start. I won't let you pressure our baby to succeed. Nothing good comes from it."

"But I can watch documentaries with our child. What musical instrument do you think? Cello? Violin? What about the trumpet? I always wanted to play the trumpet."

"The trumpet!" she chortled. "Since when did you want to play any instrument, let alone the trumpet?"

Not responding, I changed tactics. "Fisher Price has apps for babies."

Sarah set her fork and knife down methodically, taking extra time to weigh her words. "This coming from the woman who had a flip cell phone when we started dating."

She leveled her gaze at me, and I felt my confidence wilt. I put my palms up. "Okay, okay. I give. But some of them seem harmless, like the animal sounds."

"Lizzie, I'm not opposed to learning tools." Her voice was even but firm. "I'm opposed to pressure and setting unreal expectations."

"So I guess the *Learning Letters Monkey* app is out?" I flashed my cell phone.

"Let me see that," she demanded. "How many apps have you downloaded? You do know I'm not even pregnant yet, right?" We were to attend another appointment with the doctor next week.

I rubbed the crease that formed in the center of my forehead. The other day, I had downloaded a ton of those apps on my phone to try them out. Of course, then I realized the baby would need a tablet, too—thank God I hadn't said that out loud.

"I get it. You need distractions. Maybe you should sign up for a hobby or something."

"A hobby!" I scoffed.

"I'll buy you a trumpet." Sarah pretended to dangle what I assumed was a trumpet in my face.

"Deal!"

"One condition, though. You have to practice when I'm at work," she smirked.

"Really! I hope you're more supportive of our child." I raised an accusatory eyebrow.

"I'm hoping our child is more mature than you."

I feigned hurt. "Is it too childish to share a dessert?" I nodded to the table behind her. "The brownie sundae looks very tempting."

* * *

Ethan was sitting at our usual table in Starbucks. The door closed behind me, shutting out the street traffic. He didn't bother looking up from his novel. *Usual table*, I'd thought, as if we still met once a week, like we used to before Casey came along. Before I got married. Before. Before—when life seemed miserable and yet less complicated. I fucking hated irony.

I ordered a chai from the young man behind the counter. He looked like he wasn't old enough to drive a car. How was it that young people were starting to look younger and younger while I felt and looked older with each passing second? Earlier that morning, I'd plucked two black hairs from my chin. Seriously, no one warned you about that becoming the norm.

I strolled up to the table.

"Howdy, stranger." Ethan set his book aside.

"Imagine meeting you here," I replied.

He smiled his cynical smile, his thin moustache giving a quasi-intellectual appearance. The Coke-bottle glasses he always wore added to the effect. "I haven't been to a Starbucks in years, not since you."

"My, you do know how to charm a girl," I winked. "Who

knew I had the power to ruin Starbucks for you. Me, I still pop in every day. I'm addicted to this." I raised my chai and took a melodramatic sip. "I wish I could kick the habit. It's wreaking havoc on my girlish figure. Just the other day, my thighs rubbed together. I felt like a stuffed pig."

"Are you riding much lately?"

"I try to get out for short rides each day, but I don't seem to have enough hours in the day, and it feels wrong to be riding and doing something I enjoy."

He nodded, but didn't ask why. I sensed Ethan knew that even better than I did. He usually knew what I was feeling long before I processed it.

"Who called you?" I tucked a flyaway strand of hair behind my ear. My hair was thinning, random strands slipping from my ponytail no matter how tight I made it.

"What do you mean?" He looked away.

"Sarah or Maddie?"

Ethan threw his hands in the air. The jig was up. "Both, actually. I'm not sure if they planned it that way or whether it was just a coincidence."

"There aren't any coincidences when it comes to those two."

"You have to admire their methods. I'm still amazed they got you to wear a wedding dress. A white one!" he hooted.

I cringed, recollecting. "Don't remind me, please."

"And the cake. Did you know Sarah intended on smearing the cake all over your face?" His eyes sparkled over the disgraceful memory.

I crossed my arms and huffed. "She promised me she wouldn't."

Ethan cocked one eyebrow. "And you believed her?" he tsked. "Seriously, I would have thought being a woman would have given you a better advantage in a lesbian relationship."

"So, what's your mission today?" I tried to steer the conversation away from our wedding. I hated being the center of attention; even the memories of having to be a "bride" gave me gooseflesh. I'd cried during my toast. How humiliating!

"To see how you're doing. You know, the usual with you. Do you plan on running away, like normal? Or do you plan on pretending nothing is wrong and bury yourself in work?" He motioned to my bag. "How many books do you have in there?"

"Seven, but I went to the library on my way here," I defended myself.

"Why didn't you leave them in the car?" Ethan rubbed his chin and squinted: his best hard-boiled detective look.

"I planned on thumbing through them after … " I pointed to him.

"Is it option two, then?" He grinned, but I could tell he was concerned.

"Is there an option three?"

"Such as?"

"I don't know, yet," I confessed.

"Honesty—that's new."

"Anyone tell ya you're a riot?"

"Come on, I'm just teasing you. Tell me, how do you feel?"

"I'm assuming we're talking about my mom."

"That would be a good assumption. Stop stalling." He waggled a finger in my face. "And while you're at it, I've also been asked to wheedle out how you feel about having a kid, during all this."

"How did I miss that one?" I smiled, but I meant it.

"You should have left the books in the car. We're going to be here a while."

I stood. "What can I get you?" I motioned to his nearly empty cup.

"Just coffee. No frills."

Despite all of the options, Ethan always went for the house blend. Before heading to the register, I added, "I've missed our chats. Thanks."

"Don't try to sweet talk me. I'm going to get you to open up. I'm afraid of those two." He folded his arms, but the twinkle in his eyes said he felt the same.

I shook my head in mock disdain and left to order. Ethan immediately returned to his book. A man after my own heart. No wonder we got along so well.

When I returned, he held his finger up to silence me, and then traced the words near the bottom of the page. Peeking over, I saw that he was finishing up the chapter.

I set his coffee down and spread out the sandwiches and fruit I'd bought.

"Good Lord, you planning for the end of the world?" He snatched up a grape and popped it into his mouth.

"I figured it was the least I could do, since my wife and Maddie pretty much threatened your life if you didn't accomplish your mission. Hopefully this isn't your last meal."

"Let's get to it, then. What thoughts are rolling around in that empty noggin of yours?"

"If it's empty, how could I have any thoughts?"

Ethan shook an apple slice in my face. "Stop stalling. I have my own woman at home who'll kill me if I'm gone all day."

I rubbed my eyes, applying too much pressure, causing flashes of light. "Where do I start? I feel guilty, sad, relieved, angry ..." I made a circular motion with my hand. The list was endless.

He latched onto one word. "Relieved?"

"Yeah. That one goes with guilty. The most obvious aspect is that I don't want Mom to suffer anymore. But there's a part of me that is relieved. Even if we haven't talked in a few years, the threat was always there. Mom could pop back up into my life at any moment and continue tormenting me. I know that sounds heartless. I can't believe I'm mentioning it to you." I shielded my eyes with one hand, stopping myself from seeing the expression on his face.

Ethan didn't speak for several moments. Finally, he

cleared his throat. "That's why you're beating yourself up? Lizzie, when are you going to realize that you're human, just like the rest of us?"

I uncovered my eyes. "So this is normal?"

"Yes. People are selfish. It's normal. Let's face it, your mom wasn't the best. Is it right to feel this way? Well, that's a different question." He drummed his fingers on the tabletop, lost in thought.

"So it's normal, but not right. You and your riddles." I smiled weakly.

Ethan straightened in his chair, such a skinny, awkwardly tall man. "I think you need to have a come-to-Jesus talk with your mom."

"What the fuck does that mean?"

"I think you need to tell her how she made you feel all those years."

"You want me to confront my dying mother and tell her she was a crappy mom. Sarah wants me to tell her that I love her. What if I don't want to do either?" I was testy, and my voice did nothing to hide it.

"Then you'll never have peace," he stated bluntly. "And while you're at it, tell Peter he's an ass." He smiled, attempting to soften the blow with humor.

"You should meet his new fiancée. She thinks Hawaii is a foreign country."

"It should be."

I looked up from the sandwich I was about to bite into. "What?"

"We stole it. It should be autonomous."

"Jesus, Ethan, do you really think Tiffany—who pronounces her name *Tie-Fannie*—understands that much. And if we went by your logic, none of the US should be the US. Ever since—"

He raised his hand to silence me. "There's the Lizzie I know. I have one more question for you. How do you feel about Sarah and the baby?"

Without thinking, I blurted, "That's the only thing in my life that makes sense right now."

Ethan slapped the table. "Mission accomplished!"

"When do you have to report in?" I teased.

He eyed his watch. "Fifteen hundred hours."

"You're a nerd. What book are you reading? It's massive."

"*Gone with the Wind.*"

I rolled my eyes. "And you wonder why everyone in grad school thought you were gay."

"Narrow-minded assholes," he growled. He chomped off half of his sandwich and patted his mouth daintily with a napkin.

"How's the little one?"

"She said her first curse word the other day." He swallowed, and then grinned mischievously. "It was one of my proudest moments."

"What'd she say? Fuck?"

"Please, my child isn't a commoner like you. *Merde.*"

"I told Sarah *The Little Mermaid* wasn't good for children!" I shook my head.

"Sarah told me you studied the movie for days, just so you could show up my daughter. Then, when she didn't dress as Ariel again, you lost your nerve. Really, Lizzie, are you that competitive?"

I sniffed. "I don't know what you're talking about."

"Yeah right." He shook his head. "You do make your life a lot harder than it needs to be."

After Ethan left, I stayed to get some research done. Armed with a book and pen and paper for notes, I zoned out completely and was quite good at blocking out distractions. I was flipping through a reference text, making notes, when someone behind me cleared her throat in an obvious way, to get my attention. Something warned me about turning around, but I did it anyway.

Jasmine stared back at me.

Thank God Ethan had already left, or he would have reported this back to the girls for sure.

"Hi, Jasmine." I stood awkwardly to shake her hand.

"Sorry to disturb you." She smiled and gestured to the books.

I'm pretty sure she wasn't sorry, since she'd done her best to attract my attention.

"Please, have a seat." I motioned to the chair across from me. "How goes the research?" I asked politely. Historians, myself included, loved to talk about things most people didn't give two shits about. Primary sources, secondary sources, journal articles—it was amazing what got our hearts pumping.

Her face perked up, her timidity dissolving. "Really well. Thanks for all the tips. I actually received a book from the British Library yesterday. I was tickled pink!"

See? Who else would get excited about receiving a book from the British Library?

I had planned to get some work done, but ended up losing track of time and talking to Jasmine for more than an hour.

"Are you still at Starbucks?"

I hadn't realized how much time had passed until I received Sarah's text. Obviously, Ethan had already reported in, and she was expecting me home.

"Yes." I sent back, and continued my conversation with Jasmine.

A man ambled past, took one look at Jasmine, and stopped in his tracks. Both of us stopped talking and eyed him, waiting for him to say or do something. He flushed profusely and mumbled, "Did you drop a pencil?" He pointed to a lone pencil on the floor, about three tables away.

"Thanks, but that's not mine," Jasmine replied, dismissing him with a sweet, shy smile.

The man nodded but didn't budge, not for at least five seconds.

Once he was safely in the bathroom, I laughed. "Does that happen to you often?"

Jasmine stared out the window and shrugged. It was cute how she did it. I wanted to tell her about Sarah's reaction, but thought better of it. I could see Jasmine was already uncomfortable with the man's unwanted attention.

"There you are!" I knew, even without turning around, that Sarah had come to retrieve me. Before I had even spun in her direction, I could feel her glaring at Jasmine, who in turn, wilted.

I popped out of my chair and announced cheerfully, "Look who I bumped into after Ethan left. Sarah, I'm sure you remember Jasmine." Maddie strutted through the door, Doug right behind her. I swallowed a groan.

"Jasmine, I want you to meet two of my dearest friends, Maddie and Doug." I turned to the couple. "Jasmine is pursuing her PhD in history, and we both focus on children under the Third Reich." I gave Maddie a steely eyed glare, cautioning her not to be her usual self. Jasmine wasn't comfortable at all.

Doug immediately pulled up a chair next to the young woman until Maddie's cough alerted him that he should first grab a chair for Maddie. Taking his lead, I pulled out a chair for my jealous wife.

Sarah sat down stiffly. I affectionately slid my hand onto her leg, which calmed her down some. "How's the research coming along, Jasmine?" she asked, almost kindly.

Jasmine smiled but said nothing. Doug was actively gaping at her. Maddie was staring at Doug as if she wanted to throttle him. It was time for me to step in.

"Jasmine was just telling me about a book she discovered, a diary that hadn't been published when I was in school. Thanks to Jasmine"—I turned to Sarah—"and to you, I already ordered it on the iPad you got me for my birthday." I turned back to Jasmine. "I can't wait to read it. So, you really think this will change your thesis?"

Jasmine transformed into her confident self again. I could see she would make a great lecturer in a couple of years, once she controlled her nerves. Doug hung on her every word, and even Maddie and Sarah seemed intrigued.

When she finished, I added, "Of course, your findings may blow one of my new theories out of the water."

Jasmine started to interrupt, but I put my palm in the air. "Oh, no worries. That's what's great about scholarship. New things surface, changing the way we think. So many people think history is dead, but it's alive and kicking. Keeps us busy!"

Sarah stared at me. Blinked. Had I just witnessed my wife's realization that Jasmine wasn't a threat? I was too much of a historian to get turned on by Jasmine. The fact that I was giddy about a new diary rather than about the hot woman sitting opposite me didn't help my cool factor, but it did make my wife almost laugh in my face with relief.

Doug, on the other hand, was still in for a long night. I pitied him.

Jasmine looked at her sports watch. "Oh no, I'm late." She gathered her bag and reusable coffee mug. "It was so nice meeting all of you." She rushed off before Doug could hop up to give her a hug. He seemed disappointed, but no doubt that was for the best.

Maddie whacked his leg as soon as Jasmine was out of sight. "Really! Really, Doug!"

He stuttered, "Wh-what?"

"And Sarah thought I was bad." I laughed. "I only had tea with her and talked about Nazis. You were practically drooling, dude."

Doug looked betrayed, as if I should have his back. I felt bad for him, but I wasn't going to join ranks with him on this. Not when it was such a thorny subject in my marriage.

"I don't know what you're talking about." He jumped up and rushed to the bathroom.

"You want me to take him out back and give him a beat

down?" I asked Maddie, feigning some boxing jabs.

She laughed. "I would love to see you try."

When Doug returned, Sarah and Maddie were chatting about a new restaurant they wanted to try. They were becoming quite the gourmands. I blamed cable television. They really like the show *Man V. Food*: the one with Adam Richman, who entered all of these crazy food challenges, like eating dozens of oysters in thirty minutes. Yuck!

Doug took his seat tentatively. I gave him the "You're in the clear" look, and he sighed and put his arm on the back of Maddie's chair. She harrumphed playfully before turning to pat his cheek and continuing her conversation with Sarah. But the look in her eye suggested Doug wasn't completely out of the woods.

* * *

The drive to see my mother was way too short. As I neared her home, a pressure tightened in my chest; I feared it would strangle me before the day's end. What did you say to someone who had decided not to continue the fight? I couldn't blame her. Her pain and suffering must have been overwhelming. And the chemo wasn't working. I couldn't picture my mother searching for alternative treatments.

Instead of taking her to appointments, lately I had been keeping Mom company a few times a week. Was that what she wanted? Would Peter take any shifts? Or was Mr. Important still too busy?

I sighed. Jesus, I needed to get a grip. Who cared about Peter? I needed to move on. I was pretty sure Peter wasn't sitting around thinking about me.

My mother's nurse opened the door.

"How's she doing today?" I asked.

The nurse pursed her thin lips together. "She's comfortable, for now. That's all we can do."

"What do you mean?"

"She's signed a DNR," the nurse explained, putting her

hand on my arm and giving it a gentle squeeze.

"DNR?"

"Do not resuscitate. It means we won't intervene if she stops breathing or anything."

"So you just watch her die?" I was appalled by the idea. Wasn't that against their oath?

The woman squeezed my arm again. "It's your mother's wish."

She tried to walk away, but I stopped her. "Does my father know about this?"

"Of course. I know this isn't easy, but there's nothing you can do." She strode to my mom's bedroom and motioned for me to go inside.

I wasn't sure what to expect. It had been just days since I last saw her, and I knew cancer wouldn't take her easily. It wanted to make her suffer. I knew it could take weeks or months to kill her. It was just a waiting game now.

Mom sat in a recliner positioned in a sunny spot in the bedroom. I almost laughed—a recliner! Not once had Mom ever bought a recliner. It must have been a punch to the gut when she realized she needed one, or had my father or the nurse surprised her? I hoped the latter, at least that would preserve some of her dignity.

Her eyes were closed, and she was listening to a novel on the Kindle. Finally, I'd found a gift Mom actually used. The nurse left us alone, and I stood motionless in the doorway. Mom looked so peaceful. I had never seen her peaceful. Maybe it was because her eyes were closed, rather than beadily searching for something or someone to shred.

That narrator was female and had a soothing voice.

"You going to just stand there?"

Mom's voice startled me, and I jumped as if I'd seen a ghost.

"I didn't want to disturb you," I mumbled, slinking into the room. "What are you listening to?"

"Some book. I don't remember the name." She waved a

hand dismissively.

It almost made me smile. She was working hard at being her normal self, but she couldn't quite muster enough rancor in her words and tone. "I need water," she croaked. She motioned to the pitcher and cup by her bedside.

Several pill bottles were lined up next to the water. At least the nurse could still give her pain meds, even if there was a DNR. I couldn't imagine babysitting my mother if she was in excruciating pain. Keeping my back to her, I asked, "Do you need anything else?" I didn't know how to ask if she was in pain. She might infer that I thought she was weak.

"No," she barked, but in a tiny voice.

I handed her the water and settled in the chair next to her. Secretly, I wished it was a recliner, too. My eyelids felt heavy. I would have loved to close them and listen to the book with her. Instead, not knowing what to say, I asked, "How's Peter been?"

"Planning his wedding. He thinks I'll be there." She stared out the window, glaring at the leafless trees.

Peter's wedding was six weeks away. So, Mom thought she had less than six weeks. Something clutched at my throat. Why hadn't I poured myself a glass of water when I had the chance? If I poured myself one now, she'd know why. I couldn't show weakness now.

Just fucking hold on, Lizzie.

"A Christmas wedding. How romantic." I was desperate to focus the conversation on Peter, and not on what was actually happening in that room—the cancer slowly eating away at her, piece by piece.

She grunted. It was hard to decipher whether she approved or not.

"Does Tiffany have a large family?" I looked around the room, as if hoping Tiffany would magically appear and answer the question herself. Deflect. Distract. I was desperate for a distraction. As annoying as my brother's new fiancée was, she did have some benefits.

"Peter always liked being the center of attention." Mom ignored my question about Tiffany.

She hadn't liked Peter being with Maddie either, but back then, she'd hid it more. Maybe Mom no longer felt like she had to hide her contempt. Just let it fly. It was a terrifying thought.

I chuckled softly, hoping it wouldn't offend her. Peter, her precious child—the one who got all her attention. I wasn't sure I could call it love. It was always difficult to associate that word with The Scotch-lady.

"You were difficult to know."

Her words pulled me out of my head. "What?" I wasn't sure I'd heard her correctly.

"Independent. Like your father. Neither of you ever needed me. Peter needed me." She talked as though I wasn't in the room.

I sat mute, my mouth open.

The Scotch-lady rolled her head to eyeball me. "I didn't know what to do with an adult-child. Mother you? Be your friend? I felt robbed."

"Robbed?" I wasn't sure I was strong enough to pursue this conversation, but the question popped out. "What do you mean?"

"Peter was the perfect little boy. Just what I wanted: smart, handsome, friendly. He loved Hot Wheels, Legos. You … you were different. I thought I would be able to dress you up. I thought you would be a little girl. A real life doll for me to play with." She looked away. "I don't know what you were. You'd never wear a dress. One Halloween, I made you a princess costume. You cried and cried when I put it on you. You wanted to be a Smurf. Brainy Smurf," she said with as much venom as possible, a sneer on her face. "You threw such a fit that it was your first and last Halloween."

Brainy Smurf. I couldn't even remember watching *The Smurfs*, let alone remember the princess costume. Had she made me a costume herself, or did she have it made? She must have had it made. How come I didn't remember any of this?

"For Christmas, I would buy you a Madame Alexander doll. Every time you saw what was in the box, you would get this pained expression on your face, but you never told me you didn't like them. You never told me you didn't like me. But I knew it."

"I didn't like you?" My voice started to rise. "What about you? For as long as I can remember, you antagonized me. The only attention I got from you was negative. Attack. Attack. Attack. And your precious boy, Peter, would join in. The two of you ganged up on me. Jesus! I was just a child." I jumped out of my chair.

"No. You were never a child. I don't know what you were. You always had an opinion of your own. Never wanted to be told anything. Never needed anything. You just ... " She shook her head, unable to continue.

"I thought that's what you wanted. For me to be self-sufficient and not need you. God knows you tortured me whenever I showed any sign of needing anything from you," I snarled, through clenched teeth.

Mom waved my words away. I was exhausting. Her eyelids drooped. Luckily, the nurse appeared in the doorway, mouthing whether it was okay for her to enter.

I nodded, feeling like an asshole. Why was I yelling at my tired and obviously in pain mother?

"How are you feeling?" the nursed asked in a singsong voice.

"I need more."

The nursed padded over to the nightstand to retrieve Mom's medicine. "Would you like some soup?"

The Scotch-lady pursed her lips tightly, like a child refusing to take its medicine. She shook her head.

I wondered whether she was eating at all. She had never been much of an eater. Before all this, scotch provided much of her sustenance.

"Maybe when you wake up, then?" The nurse waited for an answer, but never received one. She smiled brightly and left us alone again.

My mother hit play on her Kindle again and closed her eyes. I slumped into the seat and listened with her. Our conversation was done. Nothing was resolved, but it was done.

I had an insight, but I still hadn't said my peace. I wasn't sure if Mom had said all she wanted to either. Yet, try as I might, I couldn't force any more words out. What more could I say, really?

She'd made it clear I was a disappointment for her right from the start, not just because I was a lesbian, but also because I was like my father. Did she despise him that much that she had to hate me as well? Everyone always said I looked like my father. Did she see him whenever she glimpsed me? It seemed so irrational to me: to hate me for that.

All these years I had tortured myself and tried to win my mother's approval. And now I knew there was nothing I could have done. My fate was sealed as soon as I popped out. I was like him, and therefore a mortal enemy. And then, when I announced I was a lesbian, well, it really was the perfect storm.

CHAPTER FIFTEEN

The doorbell pulled me out of my stupor. I'd been standing in my kitchen, staring out the window, although my intention had been to fix some lunch rather than to stare uselessly.

I needed to pull my shit together. Seriously, people dealt with tragedy all of the time.

Stop being a pussy, Lizzie.

I swung the front door open with more gusto than I intended and almost whacked myself in the face.

"Easy there, tiger. Don't knock yourself out." Maddie sashayed in, not bothering to wait for an invite.

"Please, come on in." I bowed like a butler letting in a princess.

"I'm starving. Do you have anything to eat?" she demanded.

"Actually, I was just thinking of having lunch. Will a sandwich do?"

"I'm so hungry I might eat Hank. Where is the little bugger?"

"Probably in my office, sunning on a cushion in the window."

Maddie wandered toward my office to give the cat some love. I headed for the kitchen to fix lunch. I guessed the princess didn't plan on helping prepare the sandwiches.

When she eventually joined me, she was cradling Hank in her arms. Usually, he protested being held, but few could ignore Maddie's charm—not even my cat. He enjoyed her attention briefly before launching himself onto the counter, knocking off some papers and then scurrying back to my office.

Maddie replaced the papers and eyed me suspiciously. "What are you doing?"

"Making your sandwich, your highness." I bowed.

"I can see that, but why are you folding the pita like that?"

I stared at her. "How else will the turkey, cheese, lettuce, and tomato stay on it? You want it like a pizza?"

Maddie let out a snort of laughter. "Oh my God! Don't move! I need to snap a photo." She whipped out her cell phone. "Doug's going to love this. He thinks I'm a bad cook!" She grinned, shaking her head.

I gazed at her. What was she on about?

"They're called pita pockets for a reason, Lizzie." She dumped all of the fillings off the pita and sliced it in half before I could stop her. To my astonishment, she separated the pita, creating, well … a pocket.

"That's so neat!" I started shoving the sandwich stuffing into it.

Maddie shook her head, chuckling. "Let me guess, Sarah does the grocery shopping?"

"Yep. And we're trying to eat healthier, so she got me these for my lunches." I bit into my pita pocket. "Wow, this is much easier."

"Can we sit down and not eat over the sink?"

"Jeez, you're demanding today," I teased. I pulled two red plates from the cupboard. "What do you want to drink?"

Maddie padded to the fridge and helped herself to a Diet Coke before grabbing a regular Coke for me.

"Sarah filled me in on your latest conversation with your mom." She sat down at the kitchen table and leaned over to place her hand on mine. "I'm sorry. Really. That must have been tough to hear."

"Yes and no. I mean, it's not fun knowing I was a disappointment from the start." I took another bite of my sandwich. Since my conversation with Mom, I'd had a ravenous appetite, my body craving all sorts of food. I made a mental note to make an appointment to get my thyroid levels checked, just to be safe. Whenever my appetite seemed uncontrollable, I automatically feared my Graves' Disease had come out of remission.

I swallowed and continued. "But it was a relief to find out she didn't just hate me solely for being a lesbian or for studying history instead of going into the family biz like Peter did. Not that those two factors helped my cause." I shrugged. "At least I didn't try to be someone I thought she wanted me to be. Marry some dude and work for Dad and then find out that wouldn't have made a difference." I let out a sigh.

"That's a very mature response. I'm impressed." Maddie slurped her soda out of the can.

I flashed a sheepish smile. "Well, my therapist may have helped me realize some of those points. I would be remiss to take all the credit."

Maddie shook her head. "Remiss." She rolled her eyes. "I hope you don't make flashcards to improve your child's vocabulary. The only people I know who talk like that are you and Peter ... and I don't talk to Peter anymore." She glared at me as if it was my fault that I reminded her of him.

"Flashcards!" I snickered. "Who still uses flashcards?" I pulled my cell phone out of my pocket and showed her my word-a-day app.

She grabbed my phone. "Hir-sut-e," she said, butchering the word hirsute.

"It's pronounced *her-soot*."

"What does it mean?"

"Hairy," I said with a shrug, as if it were common knowledge.

She tsked. "Please don't turn your child into a freak."

I put both palms up. "Sarah already lectured me when she found out I downloaded a bunch of apps for the baby," I confessed.

"What kind of apps?" Maddie finished her sandwich and licked her fingers. I handed her a napkin, but she waved it away.

"Learning apps. She was okay with some, like the animal noises. But she deleted the math and vocab apps."

"You want to teach your baby math before he or she can walk? What's with you Petries? Always so competitive about everything."

"I hope we have a boy." The sentence popped out before I could control what I was saying.

"Don't tell Sarah you said that. She'll kill you. Why a boy, though? To carry on your family name?"

"No. I just don't know anything about girls."

"Lizzie, you've never said a truer statement in your life," Maddie said, before she laughed her ass off, or should I say *derriere*?

* * *

The house phone jarred me out of an uncomfortable slumber. I fumbled for the phone, wondering why I was sleeping hunched over my desk in the library. Was it night or day?

"H-hello," I slurred into the receiver.

"Elizabeth?" Peter's voice shook me awake.

"Yes."

"She's dying." I heard zero emotion in his voice.

Before I could respond, I heard a click. Peter had hung up. Why?

And why did he say, "She's dying," and not, "Mom's dying?"

Part of my job was to analyze rhetoric. Word choice was crucial to understanding and interpreting a person's motive. Had Peter been too upset to say Mom? Was he distancing himself? Or was Mom out of the picture already in my brother's path to become even greater than our father?

Sarah's footsteps sounded on the staircase and then she stormed into the library in various states of dress and undress. Tugging a shirt over her bra, she asked, "Why aren't you getting ready?"

"She's dying," I stated.

Her face softened as Sarah tugged on a pair of jeans and crossed the room to reach me. "I know, sweetie. I picked up the phone in the bedroom and heard. We should get there as quickly as possible." She leaned down and kissed the top of my head.

"Why do you think Peter said, 'She's dying,' and not, 'Mom's dying'?"

Sarah's fingernails dug into my shoulders, where she squeezed them. She was restraining herself, was my guess. She often accused me of acting like an intellectual first and a human second. She hesitated for a moment before saying, "Honestly, I don't know. But I think we should discuss it later—"

"I read somewhere recently that when someone says 'honestly,' they're lying."

"Lizzie ..." Her voice sounded tense before it died out. She dashed out of the room and returned with my jacket. I was still fully dressed.

She clutched her car keys in one hand. Without speaking, she pulled me out of my desk chair and pushed me toward the door. "Let's go." It was a command.

Neither of us said a single word during the drive. The digital clock on the dashboard announced it was three in the morning. Heavy clouds tinged the sky a vibrant rouge, and if I didn't know the time, I would have thought it was closer to sunset or sunrise, not deep in the night. Snow sprinkled the windshield but left no trace of moisture. The asphalt was bone dry. The first snow of the season usually didn't amount to much.

A hospice nurse met us at the door and led us to Mom's room.

The death room.

I cringed, hesitating before entering. This time, Sarah didn't shove me into action; instead, she gave me an encouraging nod.

My father and brother sat on either side of the bed.

Tiffany stood by the window, gazing out.

"It's snowing outside," she said, to no one in particular.

No one responded.

My father looked up and nodded hello, seeming relieved that we arrived.

Peter didn't seem relieved. He stormed out without saying a word. No words were needed.

I took Peter's seat and reached for my mother's hand, half expecting it to be cold; it wasn't.

"We'll give you a moment," my father murmured. He stood and directed his gaze to Tiffany, imploring her to follow. She finally realized Sarah and I had arrived and smiled a wan greeting before looping her arm through my father's. I didn't think I'd ever seen anyone do that to him before.

When they left, I kept my eyes fixed on the closed door, feeling trapped. Stunned.

Sarah cleared her throat. "Do you want me to leave?"

I shook my head, unable to speak.

My mother remained absolutely still. I felt the urge to place a mirror over her mouth, like they did in the movies. Then she let out a gasp that made me jump. "Jesus," I whispered loudly.

Mom stirred, and then settled back down, still not opening her eyes. The sheet moved up and down, very slowly, almost imperceptibly. At least Mom was still breathing—for the moment.

"Do you have anything you want to say?" Sarah nudged my shoulder.

I felt like I was six years old, standing in front of the

class, panicking during my turn for show-and-tell.

My mouth opened, yet no words came out.

I stood and stared out the window. The sky was still red, and I couldn't help but wonder about it. Did the universe know about my mom's impending death?

"I never got the chance to get to know you." My words were barely more than a whisper and were followed by a small, insincere chuckle that held no joy. "We lived in the same house for eighteen years, and I never felt like I belonged. Not in your world. Not in your home."

Sarah shuffled uneasily behind me. This probably wasn't what she'd had in mind, but she stayed mute.

"Did you know I used to call you The Scotch-lady?" I turned, to see Mom's response.

Of course, there wasn't one.

Sarah blinked uneasily, but I continued. "It wasn't until you got ... sick ... that I felt something. Like you letting me in ... well, as much as you could. It wasn't how I wanted it." I sat back down next to Mom and held her hand once again. "But I'll take it," I sighed. "I didn't tell you this before, because I was scared. You always terrified the shit out of me." I paused and sucked in a deep breath. "Sarah and I ... we're trying to have a baby."

I felt Sarah's hands on my shoulders. I couldn't see anything through my tears. My voice was faltering, and I knew I needed to say the rest quickly, or I would never finish.

"I learned a lot from you, Mom. Even if we didn't have the best relationship, it never stopped me from loving you."

Finally.

I'd said it.

I twisted my hands in my lap, waiting for a reaction—any reaction.

My mother remained still. I was always late in realizing my feelings. Yet, I'd said it. I would have to be okay if she didn't reply.

I sucked in some air, flinching when I also swallowed

some snot. Sarah squatted next to me, and I rested my weary head on her shoulder and flicked more tears off my face.

"Is she——?" Peter barged in. My tears stopped him in his tracks.

I shook my head.

He didn't respond, but I felt his scorn. Determination and control, the two things my brother exuded. I felt the urge to laugh in his face. To slap him, even. His bravado was useless in this situation, and I was starting to realize that it was all he had. Bravado. No human emotion. He'd never be a happy man. Or a complete one.

"Come on, Sarah. Let's give Peter some time with Mom." I resisted my desire to emphasize Mom. He wouldn't understand why. He would never understand much of anything. I'd always thought I was the weak one, the pathetic one. But I wasn't. That was Peter. And Mom.

We found Tiffany and my father sitting at the table in the kitchen nook. Tiffany looked up when we entered and hopped out of her seat. "I'll fix you two a cup of tea."

"I'll help," offered Sarah.

I sat across from my father. He grunted quietly to acknowledge me. The sky outside had turned charcoal; the snow had stopped. I searched for some meaning in that, but couldn't piece it together. Life. Death. Who knew anything, really? Probably, by the time I had it all figured out, I would be on my deathbed. Was that why Mom had started to let me in? Did she have an epiphany? Or was she terrified? The poor woman forced to rely on the one child she had never liked.

Peter ambled in, still exuding control. I glanced at my father to gauge his reaction. There wasn't one.

"I'll go sit with her," Dad said, leaving.

Peter patted him on the back the way football players did after a tough play. There was no emotion in it; he was just going through the motions.

Sarah and Tiffany sat down, cradling their teacups.

The three of us sat in silence while Peter leaned against

the window, his arms akimbo.

"We haven't sent out invitations yet ... considering ..." Tiffany flushed. "But I hope you two will come to our wedding."

That drew Peter's attention. "Tiff, family stuff really isn't Elizabeth's thing." His tone was prickly.

None of us paid him any attention.

"It'll be a small affair, actually," Tiffany continued. "Two hundred or so."

Two hundred! That was small?

Peter cleared his throat and tried to make eye contact with his fiancée. It appeared that Tiffany was intentionally shutting him out. Had something happened between them? Maybe she had caught him red-handed, and this was part of his just desserts? She seemed stronger, more in control.

"We'd love to," said Sarah.

I nodded.

I knew Peter had always wanted a marriage just like our parents', but I didn't think he understood what that meant. He scowled, his handsome face showing his frustration, but there was something else there too. I studied him out of the corner of my eye. Defeat. He looked defeated.

I sipped my tea, its warmth sliding down my throat and into my body. I reached for Sarah's hand and gave it a squeeze.

My mother died a little after midday. All five of us were present when she took her last breath. I had hoped she'd looked peaceful when it was all said and done, but she didn't. She looked tiny and alone under her blanket.

The days afterward passed in a blur. Dad asked me to help organize all of Mom's personal papers. It was the first time I had been in her study. She'd never spent much time in there, so I never thought to snoop when I was younger. I'd forgotten about it completely until my father brought it up.

In the bottom drawer of her desk, I found several historical journals. Intrigued, I pulled them out to study the table of contents. Each one contained an article I had published. Stunned, I sorted them. To the best of my recollection, she hadn't missed a single article I had penned.

Anger welled up inside me. Would it have killed the woman to have said something—just one thing to let me know I wasn't the biggest disappointment of her life. Shit! I'd tortured myself for years trying to get her approval, and spent even more years pretending her words, or lack of words, didn't cut me to the bone. And now this.

"She was proud of you."

I hadn't heard my father enter the room, and I jumped in my chair.

I rested my hand on the stack of journals, tapping my fingers so he wouldn't notice my hand was shaking.

"Your mother was a tough woman to know, and to love, Lizzie." He sat down heavily in a leather chair. "But she was hardest on herself." He handed me a tumbler of whiskey and took a sip of his own. "She didn't allow herself to feel." He raised his glass to his dead wife's honor.

* * *

"She didn't want to feel, and I couldn't stop myself from feeling too much!" I paced in my office.

Sarah sat on the edge of one of the couches. "Isn't it good to finally know the truth?"

I paused and glared at her.

She put her palms in the air and her eyes widened. "I know it doesn't take the pain away, but still ..."

I strolled over to the bar with one purpose: to pour a stiff drink so I wouldn't have to feel; it had worked for The Scotch-lady. Raising the gin bottle, I shook it in Sarah's direction. She declined a drink. The taut look on her face suggested she thought I'd had too much. I poured a generous swig and added a splash of tonic on top, not sure why I bothered.

Then I sank into a wing-backed chair and immediately

guzzled half of my drink. Its burn began, a warm, tingling sensation coursing through my body. I let out a satisfied sigh.

"Is this your plan tonight?" Sarah motioned to my glass.

"Yup!" I answered, too enthusiastically.

She shook her head in disgust and left the room, letting me wallow in my own self-pity.

The next thing I remembered was someone shouting, "You fucking idiot!"

I rubbed my eyes, confused. Did I leave the TV on? Who was shouting?

"What were you thinking, Lizzie?"

I cracked open one eye and shut it just as quickly. Sunlight scorched my retinas.

I felt a weight on the couch and someone grabbed the gin bottle I'd been cradling. I fought, until I realized it was Maddie.

"Maddie, what the fuck?" I snatched the bottle back from her.

"'What the fuck?'" she mimicked. "What did you do last night?"

I sat up on the couch, instantly regretting that decision. The room swirled and the bottom fell out. I held my head in both hands and groaned.

"Drank ... ! Drank too much." I pushed my palms into my eye sockets, trying to still the falling feeling.

Maddie sniffed loudly. "You need a shower. I'll make a pot of coffee." She raised her hand and pointed to the door. "Go. Now."

"Where's Sarah?" I asked.

"She doesn't want to be around you until you sober up. And Jesus, you reek!" Again, she pointed to the door. "Go!"

When I stumbled into the kitchen half an hour later, Maddie said, "Well, you look a little better." She walked past me and sniffed again. "And you don't stink as much." Shoving a cup of coffee into my hand, she eyed me until I sipped the scorching liquid.

"Shit! That's hot." I waved my hand in front of my mouth.

"I don't care. Drink it."

Her scowl intimidated the shit out of me, so I did as instructed, even if I wouldn't be able to taste any food for a month afterward.

She crossed her arms. "Are you done feeling sorry for yourself?"

I nodded, but Maddie didn't look convinced.

"I'll swear on a stack of Bibles to prove it," I offered.

"Yeah, right. Like that would mean anything to you. Where's your copy of Herodotus?" She bounded to the library and I stumbled after her. I watched her scan the shelves in search of the ancient Greek book, *The Histories.*

"How do you even know about Herodotus?" I surreptitiously searched the shelves for my copy as well.

"You aren't the only one with a brain. Everyone knows the Father of History." She waved my stupidity away.

"I'm pretty sure you're wrong, considering many of my students couldn't name him on their exam paper."

"Students!" She scoffed. "No one knows anything until they finish college. Aha!" She made a beeline for it from across the room. "Here it is. Okay, put your hand out."

I complied.

"Do you swear to stop wallowing and not to drink yourself into oblivion?"

I nodded.

Maddie cupped her ear. "What? I can't hear you?"

"Yes, I swear. Now tell me, where's Sarah?"

Maddie watched the book closely, as if it might burst into flames if it sensed I was lying. "Shopping with her mom," she said. "She asked me to check on you, considering ... " Maddie indicated the empty gin bottle on the floor. Her face softened. "Would you like to talk?"

"Not really." Hank wandered in and jumped into his

usual spot in front of the window, immediately grooming one of his paws. "It was a shock, really." I wrapped my arms around my chest.

"Why don't we go hiking? I know how much you love to hike in the snow."

I did. I loved being surrounded by untrodden snow, feeling like an explorer seeing a place for the first time.

"It'll clear your head." Maddie left the room to find her coat.

I smiled, feeling fortunate to have such a wonderful friend.

"*I'm awake,*" I texted Sarah. "*And not too hungover!*"

I lied about the last bit.

CHAPTER SIXTEEN

My phone buzzed. Another text.

I blew it off, since it was probably only from Maddie. How that woman found the time to text and email twenty-four-seven astounded me. An hour later, as I was shoving some sprouts into a pita for lunch, I noticed it had no caller ID. And that I'd never responded.

"Would you like to meet me for lunch?"

My jaw nearly hit the floor. Tiffany—my brother's fiancée. Why in the world was Tiffany texting me? How did she even get my number?

It wasn't like we were friends. True, we'd be "sisters" after Christmas, but I never really bought into that. I didn't like my blood relatives, let alone in-laws.

"Yes." I sent a tentative message back.

"Tomorrow???" Within a minute, Tiffany responded.

Shit!

The last time I'd made an effort to befriend Peter's soon-to-be wife, it hadn't gone over that well. Sure, Maddie and I were still friends, but my brother hadn't spoken to me since, not until I'd seen him at the hospital after Mom's cancer. He didn't know I'd made a pass at Maddie, but he knew I'd helped her escape minutes before she was supposed to walk down the aisle to marry him. I was 99.93% certain he wouldn't want me to have lunch with Tiffany.

So I agreed.

I didn't agree just to get under Peter's skin; I was also curious about what she wanted. Knowing Peter wouldn't approve was just an added bonus.

I arrived early at the restaurant the following day. Tiffany was fifteen minutes late. It shocked me. I figured she'd be the type to arrive much later.

"So sorry I'm late, traffic was a bitch."

Again, this surprised me. She didn't just apologize for being late; she spoke like we were old friends. Something was going on, and I wasn't entirely sure I wanted to know what.

"No worries. I always have a book." I patted my Kindle.

"Let me guess, you're like Peter. You arrive early for everything. Except that he spends his time answering emails, not reading." Her tone suggested she preferred my way of killing time, even if she didn't read herself. I wondered if his career was causing issues on the home front. His job was the only thing my brother was devoted to. I used to think he was loyal to my parents, but after seeing how he handled Mom's death, I suspected he was more of an opportunist than I'd thought. People didn't matter to Peter. Business mattered. That and his inheritance.

"How is Peter holding up?" I had a pretty good idea, but I thought it would be polite to ask.

She waved a hand. "You know Peter."

I did. But I wondered if she knew the man she was marrying in less than a month.

The waitress popped into view and scared the shit out of me. Was she a ninja or something?

"What can I get you two?"

I nodded for Tiffany to order first. She glanced at the menu and ordered a salad. How typical.

I ordered a steak and parmesan sandwich, with a side salad instead of fries. Sarah was really on my case lately about eating better. I'd never been a big fan of rabbit food, but I thought I might as well make an effort, especially since Sarah had been buying organic at home.

"So, you're probably wondering why I invited you to lunch." Her frown and smile baffled me.

"Uh …" Should I be honest with her? "Actually, yes I am." I decided to go for it.

"It breaks my heart that you and Peter aren't close. I plan on changing that." Her smile was shrewd; it made her look ridiculous instead of triumphant.

"Really? How do you propose to make that happen?" I lifted my iced tea.

"I want you to be one of my bridesmaids," she declared. She said it like it was the most obvious solution.

I choked on my drink.

"I knew you'd react like that," Tiffany beamed.

Was she trying to kill me?

I cleared my throat, stalling for time to figure out how to respond.

"Don't try saying no. I've already ordered your dress. I guessed at your size, but I think you'll find I'm good at guessing. Plus, you'll have a final fitting a week before the wedding." She shook her head and her blond hair fell perfectly into place. "I'm so glad we have it all worked out."

"Have you told Peter this plan?" I was finally able to speak.

"Peter?" She quirked her eyebrows. "Why would he care about the wedding plans?"

I couldn't determine whether his apathy bothered her or whether that was how she wanted it. I had a feeling this ditz was used to getting her way, no matter what. And I wasn't entirely sure she was a ditz.

"Sarah won't mind, will she?" Tiffany did her best to look concerned.

"About what?" I asked, flummoxed by the turn the conversation was taking. Shit, I was already a bridesmaid in a wedding I didn't want to attend. Now what?

"Well, you'll have to walk down the aisle with a man."
Tiffany gave a strange little smile.

Was that guilt or triumph? Was she trying to cure my
lesbianism as well?

It took a lot of effort for me to not laugh in her face. I
dug my nails into my left palm under the table, to keep myself
from cracking up. "Oh, that. Sarah won't care at all."

"Good. I didn't want to step on any toes."

I was pretty certain she didn't care about anyone's toes.

"Trust me, that's something Sarah never has to worry
about."

"You cheating, or you cheating with a man?" Her eyes
narrowed until she resembled a lioness about to lunge at its
prey.

Her question floored me. And her nonchalance was a
good indicator that she knew everything about Peter and my
father. Just great. Would she watch me too, to see if I was a
cheater? I seriously doubted she would make any effort to
protect Sarah. She seemed like the type to gather intel for her
own personal benefit.

It struck me that perhaps I had seriously underestimated
this woman from the beginning. I had thought Peter was
playing her, but maybe she had been playing him. I wished I
could call Peter to see how he was handling the situation.
Then again, why bother. I didn't even like him. Maybe this
wedding would be more entertaining than I thought.

"Also, I hope you can give a toast during the dinner,"
Tiffany said, before devouring a crouton, crunching loudly.

Fuck!

* * *

"A bridesmaid! You said no, right?" Sarah leveled her gaze at
me.

"How do I say no to that request from my future sister-
in-law?" I stared back at her, feeling helpless.

"You just say no." Sarah studied me. "Oh, God, you

agreed?" She started laughing. "Wait till Maddie hears this."

Before I could respond, Sarah left the room, dialing her cell. Not long after, she returned to the kitchen. She'd already told Maddie, and I hadn't even finished making my tea. How in the world did those two gossip so much so quickly? I wished I could be as efficient, but with my research, not my gossiping. I would be three times as productive if I were as quick as they were. I would be on my fourth book, instead of my second.

"Maddie wants me to film it all. She's taking bets that you'll fall walking down the aisle, or freeze and say something completely inappropriate during your toast."

"That second accusation doesn't seem fair. She can't give two different scenarios and count it as one." I bit into a scone.

"Is there more hot water?" Sarah gestured to my tea. I nodded.

"Fix me a cup, will ya?"

"Yes, ma'am. Anything else, ma'am?" I tried to mimic a slave's voice, but failed miserably.

"Yeah, don't talk like that." She swiveled around on a barstool, smiling.

Was it just me, or did Sarah have a certain glow about her?

CHAPTER SEVENTEEN

A string of giggles issued from the kitchen. I sat at my desk in the office, wondering if I wanted to know what Sarah and Maddie were up to. Something told me their merriment had something to do with me, so I chose to remain hidden.

I should have known it wouldn't work. I also should have installed a lock as soon as we moved in.

"I have a gift for you." Maddie burst through the office door like she owned the place, waving a garment bag at me.

Sarah waltzed in after her, looking full of herself.

"I told you to say no … " Sarah said, her words disappearing into a gale of laughter.

I stared at the garment bag, unable to think of anything to say.

Maddie shook it. "Aren't you curious to see what's inside?"

I shook my head.

"Too bad." She ripped the zipper open to reveal a hideous red and green dress, so disgustingly ugly that no woman in her right mind would ever wear it.

"What the fuck is that? Your prom dress from 1999?"

"Ha, you wish. I wouldn't ever put this thing on, not even then." Maddie's grin made me squirm in my chair.

"Three guesses? What do you think it is?" Sarah chimed

in.

"You mean besides a hideous dress?" I needed clarification.

Sarah nodded.

"Uh, something that should be burned," was all I could think of to say.

"Oh, just tell her, Sarah. I've never met a more clueless person." Maddie was doubled over with laughter.

"It's your bridesmaid dress for Peter's wedding." Sarah was enjoying herself—too much, I thought.

I snapped my mouth shut, shocked. "I'll look like a deranged Christmas gift."

"Yeah. It's like something a ninety-year-old grandmother would wear." Maddie flicked the fabric with a finger. "Not only is it ugly, it's also scratchy. I wouldn't be caught dead in it."

"I'll pay you one hundred bucks to wear it to dinner tonight," I said, only half in jest.

"Nope. You'd have to pay me a lot more than that."

"One thousand."

"Where?"

"Old Town."

Maddie scrunched up her face. "So lots of people would see me." I could see her mulling it over.

"That is the point."

"Nope. Not going to do it." She folded the dress over the back of my chair, and brushed off her hands, as though she wanted to cleanse her fashion sense.

"Your loss."

"What about two thousand?" Maddie bargained.

"No way!" Sarah waggled a finger at both of us to stop the madness. "Knowing you two, something would happen to the dress, and how would I explain that to Tiffany? She's put me in charge of you, Lizzie."

"Ah, Sarah, you're no fun," I pouted her accusation away.

"I wonder what type of shoes you'll wear with a dress like this?" Maddie turned serious.

"Maybe we should raid Mrs. Claus's closet," I offered.

Maddie snorted, taken aback that I'd uttered a joke that was somewhat funny.

Sarah tried her best to maintain her *I'm in control* bravado, but it was slipping.

How in the world had I ended up in this situation?

* * *

I tapped the side of my champagne flute with my knife. No one in the room took any notice. Actually, I think the din increased, as if everyone was intentionally giving me the cold shoulder. Any pride and confidence I had seemed to ooze out of me. I glanced to my side and caught Tiffany's attention. I had been shocked to discover that Sarah and I were to be seated at Peter's table. I thought for sure he'd stick us in the back, right next to the kid's table.

Tiffany stood and shouted, "Quiet, everyone. Lizzie wants to say something."

Shit, she was annoying. A burning sensation seemed to work its way up my neck to the top of my head. I was sure I looked ridiculous—almost as red as my dress.

I glanced over at Sarah for support. She flashed me her *you can do it* smile. At least my wife looked confident that I could get through my toast without making a total ass out of myself.

"Uh …" I cleared my throat. "Many of you don't know me … or at least …" I stepped from side to side, fighting the urge to bolt from the room. "Or, at least, you didn't know me before today, but I have a feeling many of you will remember me … or at least the dress." I pulled out the hideous skirt to emphasize my point. Laughter floated out from the crowd, bolstering my courage.

Everyone laughed, except for Peter. Even the other bridesmaids nodded their understanding. We all looked ridiculous.

"I probably should mention that I'm Peter's sister."

Some lady uttered too loud, "I didn't know he had a sister."

I raised my glass. "Now you do. How's this for making an impression?" I downed a third of my champagne.

Sarah covered her mouth. For a second, I thought she might pee herself.

The mood relaxed a little; Peter's evil glare, did not. But to tell you the truth, I was enjoying it. The man was insufferable. He didn't know how to relax, not even at his own wedding. He'd been strutting around with his chest puffed out all evening, like a conquering hero returning from war. Every time I heard his booming voice, I wanted to vomit.

"In all seriousness …" I paused not sure what to say. I glanced at Peter and Tiffany. She beamed. Peter looked his usual smug self. "I wish both of you the best." I resisted the urge to add, *You'll need it.*

My speech over, I sat down in my seat, completely relaxed. For days I'd been dreading my brother's wedding, afraid I'd screw up my toast. And I had messed it up, big time, but at least it was over. One of Peter's coworkers stood up to add his two cents. He talked about how Peter was the most astute businessman he'd ever met. Was this a board meeting? I sucked, but at least I wasn't shameful enough to stick my nose up Peter's ass.

The following day, Sarah and I joined my father, Peter, and Tiffany for brunch. Tiffany thought it'd be nice to have a family get together before the newlyweds took off for their honeymoon. Sarah had convinced me to go. I found it odd that Tiffany's side of the family didn't attend the meal.

"Sarah, I noticed you aren't drinking your champagne. It's the best they offer." Peter's haughty grin annoyed the hell out of me. Everything he ever ordered was the best—or so he said.

"I guess I'm just not in the mood for bubbly," Sarah declared.

"Bubbly." Peter looked aghast. "This is not the kind of champagne you find at your local wine shop." He shot me a reproving glare. "I bet you've never ordered champagne this divine." He took a careful sip, his expression reverent, as if he was kissing Jesus' feet.

Divine. What drug was my brother on, anyway? Divine, my ass. It tasted like champagne. Good, champagne, yes, but I wasn't having an out-of-body experience with each swig.

Sarah and I hadn't planned on breaking the news that she was six weeks pregnant. We both firmly believed we should wait at least another month. Actually, I didn't ever plan on telling Peter, not if I could help it. My hope was that Tiffany would lose interest in family time once all the wedding hoopla settled down.

"What exotic adventures do you have planned?" I tried to steer the conversation to safer waters.

Peter puffed out his chest. "I plan on eating the finest food and drinking the finest wines." He set his glass down firmly. "Elizabeth, I'm appalled that you don't treat Sarah to the finer things in life. I'm confounded as to why she refuses to try this champagne. I know for a fact she's never had anything this nice. Obviously, you two just aren't used to a life of luxury."

My father stared out the window. I couldn't determine whether he was listening. He was probably lost in his own world.

"She doesn't have to try your fucking champagne, okay," I muttered through clenched teeth. I immediately regretted my word choice, but really, he'd pushed me into it with his elitism.

Sarah put a hand on my arm, rubbing it so Peter could see it. He rolled his eyes, which I suspected was her intention. I wanted to shout, "Homophobe!"

"Peter, I'm not trying to snub you or your champagne. I

can't drink," Sarah explained.

"Can't drink!" he jeered. "That's absurd. You mean you don't want to."

Peter missed the meaning behind her words—and the twinkle in her eye. Sarah was positively radiant. I hadn't ever seen her look more beautiful.

"Oh my God!" Tiffany squealed. "When are you due?" She grabbed both of Sarah's hands and swung them about as if she was playing an accordion.

Women had a way of picking up on these things.

Peter frowned at his new bride, both exasperated and clueless.

"We didn't plan on saying anything until you two got back." Sarah took a deep breath. Tiffany let go of her hands, and Sarah flashed me her *prepare yourself* look. "We're due in August."

Tiffany clapped her hands. "I'm going to be an aunt." She turned aunt into two syllables, and I tried to picture our child saying, "A-Unt Tie-fannie."

Realization dawned on Peter's face. It was priceless. I'm sure he never considered that we'd have a kid. And he'd probably never given two thoughts to the idea that we'd be the first to give our father a grandchild.

He scowled. He had been first with everything, yet I had beaten him to one of the biggest milestones in our father's life. Peter wasn't just miffed; he looked like he wanted to commit murder.

My father, on the other hand, turned slowly to face me and then turned to Sarah. His usual poker face carried a faint trace of glee. "Really?" he asked.

My grin answered him, and Sarah confirmed with a resounding, "Yes."

"That's wonderful." He added, almost wistfully, "My first grandchild."

His words floored me.

"August, though, so that means you're only six weeks

pregnant? Anything could happen. Isn't it too early to tell people?" questioned Peter.

Everyone ignored him. I felt pity for him. He really just didn't have a clue about life. Not surprising, really, considering who raised us. Part of me wanted to tell him it was all right not to be perfect. The other part said, "Don't bother. He won't get it."

His bride raised her champagne flute. "To new beginnings, all around!"

AUTHOR'S NOTE

Thank you for reading *A Woman Ignored*. If you enjoyed the novel, please consider leaving a review on Goodreads or Amazon. No matter how long or short, I would very much appreciate your feedback.

You can follow me, T. B. Markinson, on twitter at @50YearProject or email me at tbmarkinson@gmail.com. I would love to know your thoughts.

ACKNOWLEDGMENTS

I would like to thank my editor, Karin Cox. I am extremely grateful for all the hours she spent hunting for my mistakes, and for her patience, insight, and guidance. Thank you to my beta readers, who assisted me in the early stages. Jeri Walker-Bickett, proofreader extraordinaire, it gives me much peace of mind to hit publish after you have combed through the manuscript. Erin Dameron-Hill designed a beautiful cover, for which I'm truly thankful. Lastly, my sincerest thanks go to all my blogging buddies who have cheered me on for the past four years. When I first heard of blogging I scoffed thinking I would never take to it. It wasn't until I met so many wonderful people online who have been there for me through the best and worst times did I realize how wrong I was. I'm honored to call of you my friends and I'm so thankful I changed my tune about starting a blog.

ABOUT THE AUTHOR

TB Markinson is an American writer living in England. When she isn't writing, she's traveling the world, watching sports on the telly, visiting pubs in England, or taking the dog for a walk—not necessarily in that order. She has also written *A Woman Lost*, *Marionette*, *Confessions From A Coffee Shop*, and *Claudia Must Die*.

23334146R00128

Made in the USA
San Bernardino, CA
14 August 2015